Quarry Face

Karen Mitnick Liptak

Copyright © 2017 by Karen Mitnick Liptak

All rights reserved.

Cover photograph of the quarry © by Peter Aaron

Cover photograph of the flower © by Fritzflohrreynolds (Own work)
CC BY-SA 3.0 via Wikimedia Commons

No part of this book may be reproduced in any form or by any electronic or mechanical means including information storage and retrieval systems, without permission in writing from the publisher.

Printed in the United States of America

First Printing November 2017

ISBN 978-1-64136-285-6 Paperback

Published by: Book Services
www.BookServices.us

Dedication

To Jana, who instinctively knows things hard to believe, and to all those on Earth who intuit "there must be more."

Contents

1. Getting To Know Me 1
2. The Sign 11
3. First Contact............................18
4. A Vision, Then Frogs......................26
5. The Skinny One 34
6. The Question 46
7. Who *Are* You? 56
8. Why Not Erik?............................70
9. Jimbo's Jolt 84
10. The Jerk................................92
11. War & Peace............................105
12. Quarry Starry Quarry 114
13. Eve of Destruction.....................126
14. Welcome To Carmel 133
15. No Trespassing, Take Two 137
16. A Matter of Time.......................146
17. Arrow of Time 150
18. Last Launch 156
19. A Smudge & A Glimpse 169
Epilogue 180
About the Author...........................191

Chapter 1
Getting To Know Me

Birds of a feather
Flock together
In chirps to chatter
About light matter.
   Jolie Rich
   Carmel, New York

I'd probably faint if a bird answered me.

And not because that'll mean I've got psychic powers. I don't think anyone does, not really. Psychics I see on TV look like performers to me. But, and this is embarrassing, ever since last week when we got up here to Carmel, I've felt I have to try mentally talking to birds. It's so weird. I stopped playing around with ESP after what happened in third grade, which I'd rather not mention. But now I've got this weird feeling that I should try again, only with birds, not humans, which makes sense, considering what I still don't want to talk about.

Oh, and by Carmel, I mean the town in upstate New York. When I first told my friends in Brooklyn I'd be spending the summer in *Carmel*, helping Mom house-sit for Aunt Tish, and watching Harry, most either joked that

Quarry Face

Carmel sounds like a candy, or they thought I meant the Carmel in California. When I explained I meant the one in New York, those who knew the other Carmel looked like they felt sorry for me.

I guess that's because, according to Aunt Tish, the other Carmel's beautiful, while this one's a sleepy old town with just one attraction—the quarry. She said to ask her next-door neighbor, Marco, who's a good friend of hers, to take us there when he gets back from a major photo shoot.

My aunt's favorite word lately is *major*.

I've got a *billion* favorite words. That's because I love to write. I've kept notebooks since I was eight years old, and I try to write every day, stuff like what I did and heard, and my stories, and poetry—silly, rhyming poetry. It's weird, which I guess I say a lot, but two years ago, on my thirteenth birthday, I decided I want to be a writer when I grow up. The thought popped into my head and I decided, yes, that feels right, even though Dad says that unless you get very lucky, you have to be rich in more than just name to be a writer.

I hate when he says stuff like that.

Actually, even if Mom's nice to him lately, I hate my father these days. And it's not just because he slept with his secretary at work. And it's not just because now I've got to spend the summer up here rather than having fun with my cousin, Martha. She's sixteen and a half and promised, not that I asked, to teach me about boys. I figure she's right, even if I'm not into guys yet, which I worry is probably also weird.

Oh, look, a bird's landing in Aunt Tish's vegetable garden.

Chapter 1 - Getting To Know Me

Harry's sitting near me on the front stoop, still piling up pebbles to make a hill. He's got way more patience than me. A good voice for a seven-year-old, too. He's humming "The Itsy Bitsy Spider" again and again. He'll be fine for a while. As for me, on the last page of my journal, I've got a list of my attempts to talk to birds. This one will be *Test #32. Date: July 7, 1985. Time:*

"Harry? Time?"

Harry loves telling time with his new watch. "Two twenty-one. No, two twenty-*two*."

I've got my routine down pat. I close my eyes, then clear every thought from my head until my mind is blank. Next, I concentrate very hard on imagining a beam of red light in my mind. Not easy, but I'm getting better, and when I'm ready, I send my message on that beam to the bird's ears. And it's not that I expect a response, but here goes.

Please, dear bird, if you can hear me, fly over to my shoulder right now. Please. Pretty please. Pretty, pretty, preeeeeetttttty please.

I count to 20 like usual. I open my eyes. The bird's paying me no mind, just pecking at the soil. *Test #32. Date: July 7, 1985. Time: 2:22 P.M. Result: Negative.*

I wonder what kind of bird it is. It doesn't look special, just a plain brown bird. The bird probably thinks the same about me. *She's just some plain brown-haired human.* I wouldn't mind being unique, of course. But when I look in the mirror, I see this very plain girl with big brown eyes, a lot of freckles, a small nose Grandma says I should be grateful for, and ears that are a bit too big. Also, good teeth, thanks to them spending three years behind metal bars. Also, long brown hair often worn in braids. That's me, your run-of-the-mill high school sophomore-to-be.

What's that? Rustling? Harry heard it, too. We both turn towards the bushes. A second later, there's a tall, thin man with curly black hair and a bushy black beard pushing aside the bushes between Aunt Tish's cottage and the big house next door and heading towards us. A camera is bobbing on a strap around his neck. I've got to smile. Aunt Tish said her neighbor never goes anywhere without his Nikon. He looks in his early 30s, like my aunt, to me. And his scraggly beard reminds me of her boyfriend's, except Chuck's is blond.

I'm standing on my stoop before he reaches us. He's very tall.

"You're Marco Goodman, aren't you?" I say with a smile.

"Right you are. I just got back and found your aunt's note in my kitchen. She says you guys are house-sitting here with your mom."

"She told us all about you, too. She said you're the best photographer she knows," I reply.

"Really, Tish said that?"

He sounds surprised. I like that. I hate people who act arrogant because they're talented. I think talents are gifts to be grateful for. Like, I love to write, but I don't know if I'm talented enough to call that a gift. If it were, I'd be forever grateful.

Chapter 1 - Getting To Know Me

Marco's peering at Harry. "Let's see, you must be Harry, and what are you, ten years old?"

Harry snorts a giggle and holds up seven fingers. "No, silly, I'm seven!"

Marco laughs. His teeth are very white. I bet he doesn't smoke like our dad.

"I'm Jolie, in case you didn't guess. And I'm—" I close and open my fist three times.

Marco laughs some more. I like getting laughs.

"Jolie? That's a pretty name. Are you guys French?"

"French! If you talked to us much longer, you'd know we're from Brooklyn. But Aunt Tish found my name in a book of baby names and my parents liked it."

"Well, Jolie means 'pretty' in French. It suits you very well," Marco says.

I like compliments like everyone else, but I *hate* how much looks matter. Besides, he's probably just being nice. Oh, look. The bird I tried talking to is leaving. There he goes. It must be wonderful to fly. Bye, bye bird.

"According to your aunt, she and Chuck are shooting a documentary in Yugoslavia. A place called—how do you pronounce it, anyway?" Marco asks.

"It's pronounced Med-ju-gor-e-a. But it's spelled M-e-d-j-u-g-o-r-j-e," I tell him.

"Never heard of it. I'll check my world atlas later."

Quarry Face

"Aunt Tish says it's a very, very small town," I say, sitting back down, my braids swinging behind me. "They're filming six teenagers there who claim the Virgin Mary's been visiting them every day for the last four years, since 1981. They say she's bringing them messages for the world."

"Tish doesn't *really* believe that kind of stuff, does she?"

"She says she doesn't have to believe it, just let the footage speak for itself," I say, repeating what she told me. "They'll interview the kids and film them while they're seeing, or think they're seeing, the Virgin Mary. They'll also shoot other people who live there, and lots of visitors, too. Aunt Tish says people come from all over the world, looking for miracles, like being cured from a disease, or getting a job, or saving their marriage. Stuff like that. She said she'd write as soon as she finds out what's really going on."

"Let me know if she does. In the meantime, the town must be making a fortune from all the tourists," says Marco. He looks at his watch. "Hey, I'd better get back. I'm expecting some calls about work."

Harry jumps up. I start getting up again, too. Marco puts out his hand to help me. But as I take it, he gives me the strangest look, like an astronomer who sees something through his telescope he can't quite believe. We're both wearing sunglasses, but I can feel his eyes.

"Are you staring at me?"

"Was it that obvious? I'm sorry. It's just that I've been taking photos of the quarry for weeks, and they've been

Chapter 1 - Getting To Know Me

missing something I couldn't put my finger on until right now. Don't laugh, but I think it's your face."

The quarry! That's where Aunt Tish said we should go.

"Jojo's got a quarry face!" Harry giggles.

"Thanks a lot, Harry," I say, but with a smile.

"Quarry face? That's cute, but I'm serious. I'd love to shoot some slides of you there. Can I get permission to take you guys there tomorrow?"

He's looking at our front door.

"Mom's not here. She's working this summer as a cashier at Barker's Department Store in Carmel Plaza. That's 'cause we don't have a car and—"

Before I finish, Harry's tugging on Marco's hand and asking, "Hey, what's the quarry?"

I was wondering the same thing. Aunt Tish mentioned it, but never explained what it was. I'm guessing a shop in Carmel Plaza that sells rocks. Or maybe a restaurant. A mine? Harry and I both give Marco quizzical looks.

"Aha! Looks like you're both in for a treat," Marco says. "The quarry used to be an iron-ore pit mine, but after it closed, water from a nearby reservoir flooded the place, turning it into the best swimming hole in the world."

"In the world?" I ask. Shouldn't we have heard of it then?

Quarry Face

"Not convinced, are you? I bet you'll change your mind once we go there. Some people call it magical."

Harry's eyes open wide. He mouths the word 'magical' to me.

"Besides, Harry's dying to go swimming. Aren't you, mate?"

Harry pants like a lion.

"I could really use your 'quarry face' for my shots," Marco goes on. "They're for an article in a travel magazine about secret swimming holes on the East Coast, and I'm way behind schedule. What do you guys say?"

Harry looks up at me. Here come the clasped hands. He's lucky he's so lovable. My friends are always complaining about their younger brothers and sisters. I lucked out with Harry.

"Okay, as long as Mom agrees," I reply. She'll probably be glad we get to go swimming.

Marco's still smiling as he tries tousling Harry's thick brown hair. My brother hates people doing that. He swings for Marco's shoulder, barely tapping it. Marco pretends to punch Harry back, then waves goodbye and jogs off. Soon all that remains are sounds; rustling leaves and crunching gravel. When I turn back to Harry, he's already found a new activity. He's stalking a black-and-white butterfly fluttering among some bright yellow wildflowers.

Catching me watching, Harry puts his finger to his lips.

Chapter 1 - Getting To Know Me

Silly boy. I love silence so much I could start a Silence Fan Club. I don't even play music when I'm alone, which my cousin Martha says is one of a million reasons I'm a freak—lovable, she says—but a freak. Not that anyone on Earth gets total silence. Take now, for instance. We're not making a peep, but there's traffic from the highway, guys hammering down the road, and birds chirping everywhere. I once read there are 10,000 species of birds on Earth. Ten thousand! Can they all understand each other? If I finally talk to one bird, will I be able to talk to them all?

Oh, another plain brown bird's swooping down, this one where Aunt Tish planted her hybrid broccoli. Could it be the same bird as before? I can't tell, but Harry's safe and happy, so I'm going to try Test #33.

First, I shut my eyes and chase all my thoughts away. These days, I'm sure I think way too much about how mad I am at my dad and how sad I am for Mom and how unfair it is that I'm stuck up here for my fifteenth summer. I know, I know, I need a better attitude. Okay, thoughts, leave me alone. Go. Get lost! Scram!

I'm getting there. Almost. Yes, I can see that narrow beam of red light taking shape in my head. Now that it's here, I'm going to beam my message straight through that bird's ears into its mind. *Please, bird, fly over to my shoulder right this instant, so I know I'm not crazy to feel I've got to practice telepathy on birds. I've got a nice soft shoulder to land on.*

I do my 20 count. I open my eyes.

Nothing.

Maybe this is the summer I find out I'm crazy. Maybe I've always had the craziness gene, but it took my parents' separation to finally push me over the— Stop, mind! The quarry! Focus on the quarry. Harry can swim there. And maybe it'll be fun.

But magical? Yeah, right.

Chapter 2
The Sign

> Cosmic truths are revealed
> On a need-to-know basis,
> So follow the flow
> To where you must go.
> Jolie Rich
> Carmel, New York

Last night, when Marco came over to meet Mom, he said he'd pick us up around two today. It's almost four.

"I thought you forgot about us," I shout, as he's hurrying towards our aunt's garden, and Harry's hurrying towards him. I don't mind he was late. Harry and I made a game out of watering, which was fine because I'd been able to read some poetry this morning and write some, too, while Harry played on his kid's guitar, although he did get a bit antsy.

"I wanted to come get you at two o'clock, but Jojo wouldn't let me," Harry's telling Marco, as they reach me, holding hands. Then he says, "Want to know what we watered?"

And before Marco can give an answer, Harry's zooming around the garden like he's a jet plane, and shouting out the names of all the vegetables Aunt Tish planted before her Medjugorje movie unexpectedly received a grant; she wanted to leave right away, she said, before they had second thoughts and took the money back! Actually, I think it also had to do with when they could film the most tourists. Mom said that was good news for us, because it meant we could stay upstate while Dad had 'the space he needs,' as she put it, to think and decide if he really wants to be married. I overheard everything she told Aunt Tish about what happened, and how grateful she was that she'd gotten her a job this summer to keep her mind off of everything.

I knew Mom didn't want me seeing her cry, so I didn't tell her I had. Maybe I will someday, when she's old and gray. Oh, I don't like thinking stuff like that; I hate that people you love have to get old and die. Pets, too. I wish I could change the world. But I guess there's a reason it is how it is.

Aunt Tish had Chuck write the names of all the vegetables in black marker on strips of a thick, sticky gray tape she called 'gaffer's tape.' She said filmmakers use it for everything from holding up lights to patching holes in their pants. Their garden's six rows have a stake at each end with a piece of gaffer's tape to identify what was planted.

I give Harry a big hug when he's done, which he immediately squirms from, but I can see from his smile he's proud of himself.

"I'm so impressed! You got them all right," I tell him, "even the hybrid cauliflower and hybrid broccoli." I look

Chapter 2 - The Sign

up at Marco. "Aunt Tish said we should take special care of the hybrids because she never planted any before."

"But you've got all that squash."

"Acorn, and gooseneck, and Hubbard, and spaghetti, and zucchini, too! Whoo, whoo, whoo!" Harry sings. Then he takes a bow.

Marco and I both applaud. But then Marco shakes his head.

"I hate to be the prophet of doom, but I don't think your aunt's hybrids stand a chance," he says. "The squash will take over the whole garden. I've seen it happen before."

"Aunt Tish said she got planting instructions from the best garden center up here," I say, remembering her saying she followed their directions carefully.

"Look, everyone makes mistakes. But let's not waste time talking while it's still sunny out. I had a lot of phone calls to attend to earlier, but if we leave right now, we can get to the quarry in time for the twilight show."

"The twilight show? You mean a magic show?" I say.

"You'll see."

I can't help laughing. Marco's attempt to look mysterious just looks silly.

"I'm changing! I want to see the twilight show!" Harry yells, running into the cottage.

"I take it that's a yes?" Marco shouts after him, then smiles at me.

Wow. I think he genuinely likes kids. Harry needs someone like him around.

∼

"You got any kids?" Harry asks.

"Harry!" I'm curious, too, but we hardly know Marco. It's probably none of our business. That's what my dad always says: it's none of my business, whatever it is.

"That's okay," Marco says and leans slightly right in his seat to better see Harry in his rearview mirror as he drives. "No, not yet, mate."

"But you've got a girlfriend, right? I'll have a girlfriend someday," Harry says. His bouncing on Marco's back seat is making my seat vibrate so much that I've got to tell him to sit still, which it's always hard for him to do.

We're in a Volvo, by the way. I checked because Martha always likes hearing about people's cars. She says a guy's car is the window to his soul. I tell her that's nuts; it's his eyes. I bet my ex-best friend Elyse would agree with me. Her letter from Paris came today. I'm not sure when I'll open it. Maybe never. Elyse doesn't know yet that I can't be her best friend anymore.

"My girlfriend and I are sort of separated," Marco's saying when I'm done letting my thoughts distract me.

Chapter 2 - The Sign

"We're separated, too!" Harry shouts, like he's proud of the fact.

But then, he actually believed Mom about trial separations being very popular in marriages today. And he's too young to know that our father slept with one of the secretaries at his real estate office, and not just once. I didn't overhear exactly how many times, but *once* is enough. Too much! And *everyone* is *not* having a trial separation. I can't imagine Elyse's parents cheating on each other or separating. And Elyse's dad would never say he didn't want children, which I overheard mine say—and more than once. He made it sound like a joke, but I think he meant it.

I shoot Harry a glare. He zips his mouth shut with his finger. He really is a good kid. I throw him a kiss. He throws one back.

"That seems to be the style for the '80s, couples separating," Marco says.

"Well, if that's the style, it's a pretty stupid one," I say, looking out my side window. I use the back of my hand as a tissue.

"Stupid, but real," says Marco.

"It'll never happen to me," I reply without turning back. Out my window a bunch of blurry trees whiz by. *The woods are lovely, dark and deep, and I have miles…* It's weird how bits of songs and poems and other stuff I've heard pop into my head at the oddest times. I once saw a TV show about people who hoard stuff. Their homes were a mess. Will my mind be like a hoarder's home when I'm old, so cluttered with junk that all my memories will be buried too deep to find?

"Never? That's a very strong word," Marco says.

"So are 'separated' and 'divorced.' If I can't marry forever, I won't marry at all." Wow. Even if I'm serious, how can anyone be 100% sure their marriage will last forever? Mom told Aunt Tish she never thought hers wouldn't.

Without another word, Marco swerves right, and brings the Volvo screeching to a halt against a metal chain gate so fast that Harry nearly plows into my seat.

"Hey, sorry, mate," Marco says, as we both turn to face him.

Harry's rubbing his head and laughing.

"How many fingers am I holding up?" I ask.

"Ten! Ten fingers! Every finger you have!" Harry says, bouncing from one window to the other. "Hey, is this the quarry?"

"Almost. It's just down the hill behind the gate," Marco says as I glance out my front window, going from right to left.

Behind the rusted gate, I can see a whole lot of trees that I think are sycamores, which we learned about in school this year, and I see grass everywhere except for a path in the middle that I bet leads to the hill Marco says we've got to go down. Now I'm looking towards my left—

Chapter 2 - The Sign

"I need you two to lift up the gate so I can drive through," Marco's saying, as my scan ends on a weather-beaten wooden sign that's hanging from the tree nearest the gate.

Its words are in a faded, splotchy green paint, but I can make them out—

NO TRESPASSING! KEEP OUT!

Chapter 3
First Contact

> Miracles mustn't be rushed,
> Nor spirits be crushed,
> As cosmic signs near
> To lead Earthlings from here.
>   Jolie Rich
>   Carmel, New York

"Don't worry. My friends and I have been here dozens of times, and nobody's ever kicked us out. I've seen other kids here, too," says Marco, his right hand on my shoulder.

"But I don't like breaking the law. And I certainly don't want to spend the summer in jail." I'm joking, but not 100 percent.

"Me, too? They'll put me in jail, too?" Harry asks, wide-eyed.

"You're too young. They'll just take me."

"Then all I'll have is Mommy. Don't go to jail, Jojo, please don't go!" Harry says, slumping down in the back seat.

Chapter 3 - First Contact

"Whoa, whoa, whoa, mate," Marco says, moving his right hand to Harry's knee. "Nobody's going to jail. Nobody will kick us out. And just in case they try, which they won't, I'm the best protector in the world. So, don't worry, either of you."

"I wanna go swimming, not to jail…" Harry says, like he's getting confused.

Okay, okay. I grab my backpack and press down hard on the passenger seat door handle. Harry quickly gets out too. When we're in place, Harry at one end of the chain and me on the other, I count to three and yell, "*Lift!*"

We're wimps!

"This time, let's give it all we've got. One, two, three-eeee…*lift*! Marco, help!"

We're all laughing while Marco gets out of the car, motions for Harry to join me, then holds the other side of the chain and tells us, "When I say 'three,' both of you heave your side of this sucker over the top of my car and let it drop."

"Drop on your car?" I ask. C'mon. Really?

Instead of answering, Marco yells, "One, two, threeeee!"

As soon as the chain thumps on the Volvo's roof, Marco jumps back into the car and drives through. The chain clangs down, past his trunk and back bumper.

"You do this all the time?" I call out, as Harry and I run alongside the Volvo while Marco drives farther and farther in.

Quarry Face

"That's the beauty of driving an old geezer," he yells out his window.

He's like the anti-dad. Dad goes ballistic if his Chevy gets a microscopic ding that only he can notice.

Marco stops at a spot that can be seen from just a sliver of the road, and by the time we've caught up to him, he's opening his trunk. He gives Harry a deflated blue float from it. I get the air pump. He takes out a deflated red float and a towel to carry, then slams the lid shut and motions for us to follow.

"The hill's a bit steep, so hug a tree if you need to steady yourself. Just go slow and take your time," he says.

"But then we'll miss the twilight show!" Harry tells him.

My brother's memory is better than mine! But I've got more to think about.

"Go ahead of me," I tell Harry. This way, if we've got to split fast, I can grab his hand, pull him up and make a run for it.

I'm wearing sneakers, like Marco said we should, but a few times going down, I've had to grab on to a tree not to fall. These are the skinniest trees I've ever seen. I should ask Marco what they're called. He and Harry are way ahead of me. I'm only halfway down when they're already at the bottom of the hill, dropping their floats on a patch of light brown sand, like a mini beach. It's near the water, which is a deep blue color. Beautiful. I guess it'll be fun to swim.

Marco's looking up at me.

Chapter 3 - First Contact

"I'm coming, I'm coming," I shout. He needs the air pump.

"Actually, I'd like you to stop." Marco shouts up. "Stop and look around, breathe in the air, see what you think."

See what I think? That's silly. I put my left hand on the nearest tree and use my right to shade my eyes. Stinky metal gate smell. But I smell something else. It's not the water, not the dirt, not the wildflowers I see in patches. It's familiar, yet very strange. And now this is even stranger. Marco and Harry look like they're in a painting, with a gold background, and the water's glowing emerald green. Silliest of all, I'm feeling like Julie Andrews about to burst into song on a hilltop in the Alps in that movie, *The Sound of Music*.

"Marco," I shout down. "This place is alive with the sound of magic!"

I don't even know what the words I just said mean, but I swear they feel right to say because I'm feeling better than I have in weeks, maybe forever. It's like I'm being invisibly embraced by something that's assuring me I can handle whatever comes my way, *every little thing gonna be alright,* everything's an experience, an adventure that I get to write about, good or bad. Lucky me. All things good are in the air. Everywhere. I love being here.

"Welcome to the club," Marco yells back. "And you're not even in the water yet."

"Harry, watch out!" I shout. The mood's gone.

Harry jumps back from the water's edge.

Quarry Face

"Jojo, you're such a mini-Mommy!" he yells up at me.

Marco's chuckling.

"Well, he could have fallen in," I say. Harry's water wings are in my backpack. I walk faster, but not so fast I could fall.

As soon as I reach them Marco takes the pump from me and lays it on the ground.

"Let me take some shots before you go in," he says, as he focuses his camera on me. "Just act natural."

I pose like a movie star, one hand behind my head, my nose pointed up.

Harry makes finger circles near his ears. "I don't know her. She's not my sister."

"A little more natural wouldn't hurt," Marco says, laughing at us both.

"Oh, if you insist," I say. Marco takes a few more shots, then sets his camera down on a flat rock and asks Harry to help him inflate the floats. Harry's soon grinning as he presses his foot on Marco's which is pressed on the air pump. Dad always shoos Harry away when he tries to help. Is Dad with his secretary now? I overheard that she's divorced and doesn't want kids. Maybe Dad should have married *her*. Sometimes thinking sucks. I close my eyes and breathe in deeply. *Every little thing's gonna be alright.*

"Marco, what makes this place seem magical?" I ask when I'm almost done blowing up Harry's water wings. The guys are on their second float.

Chapter 3 - First Contact

"Aha. I said my *friends* think that, mainly the women. I'm not big on magic. I majored in physics, you know. But I love swimming here, and the light's great for photos. It reminds me of Paris."

"You've been to Paris?" But of course he has. Aunt Tish said he gets sent on assignments all over the world.

When he nods, I ask, "What did you love most about it? The Eiffel Tower? The cafes? The Seine? Is that how you pronounce it?"

"You did better than me with Medjugorje."

In my head, Leslie Caron is singing "I Don't Understand The Parisians" in *Gigi,* which Mom and I saw recently on TV.

"Actually, what I love best about Paris is the sky. Day or night, when the light is just right, it's magnificent." He blows a kiss in the air. "I'll bring up my slides of Paris next weekend," Marco says.

"I'd love that."

"Let your sister have the red one," Marco tells Harry when their work's done.

"And we take the blue one 'cause we're guys, right?" Harry says.

Marco nods, has Harry toss the floats into the water, then counts to three, holds his nose, and jumps in. Harry grabs his water wings from me, squishes his arms into them, and holding his nose, jumps in, too. Meanwhile, I've started butt-bumping down three slippery rock steps.

Quarry Face

"Is she *always* like this?" Marco asks Harry. He's holding the blue float steady for my brother to climb on.

"Yup," Harry says with a grin. "She hates getting cold."

"Sorry, but—" Before I can finish, I slip and go down under. By the time I surface, the guys are laughing hysterically. But I don't care.

"This water is wonderful!" I say, amazed. I feel hugged, not cold at all. "Marco, everyone should swim here. The real crime is that the quarry's private property."

Marco's laughing as I grab the red float he's pushed towards me. He motions for Harry and me to follow. Harry paddles his float until he's behind where Marco's swimming. I hope Marco isn't mad, but I want to go the other way.

My float feels like it's gliding over a smooth glass surface as I pass boulder after boulder filled with holes holding metal rods. I guess that's got to do with the mining. The boulder I'm nearing now is different, though. It doesn't have holes or rods, just a white flower in the center with sunlight surrounding it, kind of like a halo. Lovely. But flowers don't grow on stone, silly. Do they? I want to see it up close.

Squeezing my float into a crack so it won't drift away makes me shiver, but I'm okay when I sit down next to the flower. I don't know what it's called, but it's pretty. And with water from my bathing suit fanning out around us, we're like the only survivors on a desert island.

TALK TO THE FLOWER LIKE YOU TALK TO BIRDS.

Chapter 3 - First Contact

What was that? It sounded like a voice in my head, but not *my* voice, like a thought would be. And what it's asking is silly. Birds never answer me, so now I should try ESP on a flower? Isn't that asking for disappointment?

TALK TO THE FLOWER LIKE YOU TALK TO BIRDS.

There it is again, that strange thought. Or voice. What should I do?

Harry and Marco are across the quarry, splashing each other and laughing. As long as Harry wears his water wings, he'll be okay. I guess playing along won't kill me. Embarrass me if anyone asks what I'm doing, but not kill me. Okay, here goes.

I close my eyes like when I bother birds. Wow. It's never been this easy to clear my mind. And now I'm focusing my energy on forming a narrow beam of red light. Yes, it's coming, it's almost— It's here. Okay, now I'm ready to send my message. And because I don't expect a reply, I won't be disappointed when I don't get one.

Hi, flower. You speak English?

MOVE ON.

Without being told, I know not to open my eyes. Instead, I squeeze my eyelids tighter shut and as sunlight dances on them, the beam of light I used to send my message is gently moving me on, towards where that mysterious voice came from, and I'm no longer in charge, I'm being led.

Chapter 4
A Vision, Then Frogs

> Scared of the sacred,
> Slaves to time,
> Most miss hearing
> The secrets in rhyme.
> Jolie Rich
> Carmel, New York

You're back so soon?

That first voice I heard was deep and commanding, a man's voice. This one's playful, a young girl's. But nobody else is here. Nothing's here. I'm at the end of that light beam and there are no trees, no flowers, no buildings, just a tan color all around and sand at my feet that kicks up sparkly fairy-like stardust. This is weird. I feel light and airy, like I can fly, and like I'm inside my brain but also far, far away, somewhere I can't remember ever being, yet feels like home, my real home, where I belong. Hey…a bunch of blobs are headed towards me. They're all gray, but not scary, like monsters.

Mostly, they remind me of nebulae I saw on a TV special about astronomy that I watched for science class last year. 'Nebulae' were what scientists called the blobs they

Chapter 4 - A Vision, Then Frogs

observed with their telescopes, until an astronomer named Edwin Hubble (which rhymes with bubble and trouble, so I'll *have* to put him in a rhyme sometime) figured out around sixty-five years ago that a lot of them were galaxies; collections of stars, like the Milky Way. Before that, people thought the Milky Way was all there was, there was no more. Now we know it's one of at least 100 billion galaxies in the universe. Imagine what we'll know sixty-five years from now. Maybe we'll find there are 100 billion universes. Who knows?

The blobs are getting closer. Is this a dream? Heatstroke? Did I fall through a rabbit hole, like Alice in Wonderland, except mine's invisible? I feel like I've got to keep my eyes closed if I want to stay here and I do. I feel even better here, wherever *here* is, than in the quarry. I just want to know where I am and how I got here.

A blob not far from me has started wildly spinning, like an Olympics figure skater, faster and faster until it stops and reverses its spin, slower and slower until it looks like a girl, a human girl around ten years old. She's very cute, although I hate looks mattering. She might be Caucasian or a light-skinned African-American or Asian or Native American, or something else. It's hard to tell. She's shaking her head, like she just got off a carousel ride. Her hair's long, straight, and black, and her flowing white gown looks like it belongs on *Star Trek*. Or in the Bible. At least she looks human. It's harder to talk to a blob. She's staring at me with the kind of grin I used to have when I knew a big secret I couldn't tell.

Now she's shrugging. *Oh, I thought you were... never mind. I get them mixed up.*

Quarry Face

Who did you think I was? And who are you? Or what are you and how did you get inside my brain? I'm talking mind to mind. I'm using mental telepathy. I just don't know to whom I have the pleasure. The girl's coming closer. Amazing how she looks like so many nationalities, but so what, she was a blob seconds ago! Or else I'm going crazy.

Are you from Earth, too? she asks, sounding amused.

Yes, of course I'm from Earth. Where else would I be from?

I knew it! But you've come too soon. How did you get here?

I was sitting on a rock and thought I heard someone tell me to talk to the flower next to me. And when I did that, I wound up here, but you're really a blob, so why am I even talking to you, and where am I, and what's going on?

Don't you like surprises? the girl asks. Her expression makes her look like both a wise old woman and a smart aleck in a child's body. *But I'm serious that you can't stay. You're way ahead of schedule for your species.*

I press my hands down hard. Yes, I'm sure of it. I'm sitting on a rock in a swimming hole called the quarry in Carmel, New York, USA, Earth, Solar System, Milky Way Galaxy, Universe. But my mind is somewhere else. Aunt Tish warned Mom that Harry and I might have problems because of the separation. So, have I flipped out? Or did I really enter some other dimension? Isn't that just in science fiction?

Chapter 4 - A Vision, Then Frogs

It'll be fun to get to know you someday, but you've got to go back for now, the girl tells me.

I squeeze my eyelids tighter. *But you're in my mind, I have a right to know who you are and where I am. That's only fair.*

Oh good, feisty and funny! I like that. Learn to rhyme. We love good rhymes, the girl says. Then she takes off running.

I start racing after her as if my thoughts had feet. Running feels wonderful. I've wanted to run like this ever since I found out about Dad's cheating. I'm hot on the girl's trail now. She's pretty fast, but I'm gaining on her. I'm almost where I can reach out and grab her…

WHAT'S GOING ON HERE!

I nearly crash into the girl, who nearly crashes into a shimmering blob that's speaking as it transforms into an old man. A nice old man. He's got wise, twinkly eyes and he looks like the kind of grandfather I wish I'd had. Both mine died before I was born. He's got that same every-nationality look, and his white robe, like the girl's, looks both ancient and futuristic.

I thought she was you-know-who, and even though she's come through, she's not ready, the girl answers. *She said someone told her to talk to a flower and when she did, she wound up here!*

Grandfatherly Figure smiles, like he thinks the girl sounds cute.

Quarry Face

ERMA, SEND HER BACK. YOU KNOW HOW TO DO IT, he tells her. His booming voice makes me think 'kind thunder.' He looks my way. *I'M SORRY, CHILD. IT'S TOO EARLY. BUT WE WILL SEE YOU SOON AGAIN WHEN HISTORY ENDS.*

The next instant, he's gone. I quickly turn to the girl he called Erma.

She shrugs and says, *Sorry.*

My eyelids pop open.

I'm back in the quarry. Marco's dragging Harry on the blue raft right up to my boulder, while a strange bellowing sound is coming from every direction. Maybe there really is a quarry monster. Or hundreds of frogs.

Marco puts his finger to his lips, then helps steady my float after I throw it back into the water. Crawling onto it from the boulder is easy. The bellowing's getting louder. Must be frogs. I don't see any. Did I imagine everything that just happened?

"Look, over there," Harry shrieks.

Twigs are shaking, but no frogs.

"Huh? Where'd the frogs go?" Harry asks.

"They're just warming up," Marco says, his deep voice tucked into a singsong whisper. He puts his finger on his lips again and points.

I see a frog. Now I see twenty. Wow!

Chapter 4 - A Vision, Then Frogs

They were camouflaged before, but now I see frogs everywhere, bulging eyes and pulsating vocal sacs in every direction. They're in the water on rocks and twigs and leaves and wherever I turn there are more. Amazing how I couldn't see any, but after I spotted one, a zillion more came into view. And what a noisy symphony they make!

Maybe they're all secretly Prince Charmings that a mean witch has cast a spell over.

"It's so magical," I whisper, although what I really want to say is, "Marco, did strange things ever happen to you on that boulder I was on?" But I won't. What if he thinks I'm nuts?

What if I am?

Marco raises his hands like he's framing my face for a photo.

"Oh, don't," I say and look up and away, which is how come I spot two boys maybe a bit older than me on the sliver of road above. They're standing next to their bikes and staring down at us. The skinnier one's cute, not that looks matter. Okay not that looks *should* matter.

"Hey, a jumping frog! And another! Look! Look!" Harry suddenly starts screaming.

I manage to shield my face just as dozens of frogs dive into the water all around us. When all is calm again and I take my hand down, the boys are gone.

I'll see The Skinny One again. He belongs in my story.

Quarry Face

Okay, now where did *that* thought come from? It felt like telepathy, but in *my* voice. I'll write down everything in my journal tonight. Sometimes things make more sense when I see them in writing.

"You're hearing bullfrogs trying to attract a mate. They do it every night at twilight around this time of year," Marco explains.

He sounds sad. Maybe he's thinking about his girlfriend.

He clears his throat, then adds, "Hey, it's time to head back. I promised a friend I'd give him a ride back to the city."

"I was hoping you could take us back here tomorrow," I tell Marco, as he turns Harry's float towards the shore.

"Sorry, Jolie. I've got a shoot scheduled for the next few days. It helps pay the rent up here. I mean, that's how the world works."

"Well, it's a—"

"—stupid world," Marco finishes. Then he laughs. "If you can figure out how to change it, be my guest."

"Okay, I will," I joke back, like I'm accepting his challenge, as I paddle along behind the guys. It's weird, but I want to leave here as much as I want to stay. It's like I've got to get away to think clearly about what happened here today. Did I really go somewhere in my mind and meet blobs that turned into humans and said history's going to end?

Chapter 4 - A Vision, Then Frogs

Marco and Harry reach the shore much faster than me. I grab Marco's hand. That's weird. Those kids in Medjugorje that Aunt Tish is filming just popped into my mind. Is this what's happening to them? But they weren't taken somewhere, like me. And the Virgin Mary wants to talk to them. Here, I got sent away. What did they say? I'd come too early? I must have imagined everything. But it seemed so real.

"You ready?" Marco asks as I finish tying the laces on my sneakers.

I nod, unable to make myself ask him about that boulder, that flower. What if he thinks I'm crazy? Or Mom. I wouldn't want her to start worrying. She's got enough on her mind. But I've got to know if I really met beings, whatever they are, who know about the future of the human race. I'll ask Marco to take us back here, and when he does, I'll get over to that boulder, to that white flower again. And if the same thing happens, I'll insist on staying the next time. T-i-m-e. Seems like a weird word now. Remember to r-h-y-m-e. Did I hear that? I love rhyming, so no problem there.

A shudder suddenly shakes me. In my head, with my eyes wide open, I'm seeing the old, weathered sign that freaked me out when we first got here. Its eerie green letters are vibrating in my brain, a gusty wind roaring again and again— *NO TRESPASSING! KEEP OUT!*

Chapter 5
The Skinny One

> Ask not what your universe
> Can do for you,
> But what you
> Can do for your universe.
> Jolie Rich
> Carmel, New York

"Dog breath," Harry says, then quickly puts his hands over his mouth.

Mom and I exchange smiles. He's just repeating what one of the two guys across the quarry yelled out. They're probably around my age. Maybe a bit older. And right now they're swinging into the water from a rope, scratching their armpits and screeching like apes. Good thing they're not near my boulder.

My boulder? Listen to me!

"Aren't there other places to go swimming that don't have 'No Trespassing' signs?" Mom asks, while unlacing her sneakers.

Chapter 5 - The Skinny One

Marco throws me a look while he and Harry press down on the air pump.

"Like mother, like daughter," I say with a laugh.

Marco laughs, too. So do Mom and Harry. It's nice being here together. Why didn't we get someone like Marco for a father? He *likes* kids.

"Your sister loves this place, and I meant it when I told Jolie and my mate here that nobody's going to kick us out. It would've happened long ago if it was going to happen at all," Marco says, all the while lifting his camera to his eye.

Mom quickly crosses her arms and shakes her head, which makes her curls brush across her face. "Please, Marco, don't shoot me! I look so fat these days."

"Oh, Mom, you do not!" I tell her.

I know she's trying to be funny, but I hate when she says stuff like that. It's all Dad's fault. Whenever we went swimming, he'd make the same stupid jokes about Mom's thighs looking like beluga whales. I'm sure his words hurt her, even if she laughed. I never did. As for Harry, he laughs at anything. Hopefully, he'll learn to make distinctions before someone clobbers him for laughing in the wrong place at the wrong time.

"Your daughter's right. You look fine," Marco says, as he and Harry continue inflating the floats.

"That's nice to hear, but I've been stuffing myself lately and— Oh, never mind. I'm just glad we're here," Mom says.

Quarry Face

Marco strokes his thick black curls with one hand and tells her, "You know, I always worry I'm going bald."

"Marco, you don't look bald at all," Mom says.

The sunlight's bringing out the blond streaks in her hair. Dad should have treated her better, and not just because she's cute. She's a good person.

"And you don't look fat," Marco says.

"Point well taken," Mom replies with a big smile, as she sits down and starts to dangle her feet in the water.

"Hey, this water's wonderful," she says a second later. "It's like melted butter."

"Melted butter!" Harry repeats, giggling.

"That's a new one on me," Marco says, while I make a mental note to write down what she said in my journal. Then he asks Harry to toss the floats in the water because he's so good at it.

"I'll get the red float for us," Mom tells me, before ducking into the water, and swimming away.

I'm more careful about sliding in today. I don't intend to fall. I hear more yelling from across the quarry. Hey, is one of those guys over there The Skinny One?

"Jolie!"

I turn. Click! Click! Click!

"Marco, you tricked me."

Chapter 5 - The Skinny One

Marco laughs as he lowers his camera. I do hope he gets what he needs, which he deserves for bringing us here. Aunt Tish said he's always super busy, with photo assignments all over the world. Even if Mom could drive and we had a car, I'd still want him to be with us. And not just for protection. He makes everything more fun. I just wish we weren't breaking the law.

I've almost reached Mom and the red float.

Splash!

I quickly turn at the sound. Marco and Harry are both surfacing—they must have jumped in together. I do a half turn. The guys across the quarry are staring our way. Yes, that *is* The Skinny One, the guy I saw looking down at us last week! Of course, it's not a *gigantic* coincidence, since Carmel's so small.

As I'm watching them, The Skinny One and his friend go back to fooling around. They're both screaming like apes, "Hoo, hoo, hoo!"

Is that any way for my future husband to act?

What a silly thought. Hoo, hoo, hoo to me!

Another quarter turn, and I can see Marco pushing Harry on the blue float towards us. Mom and I hold on to our float and kick our feet. Mom's got a big smile. Maybe she's feeling the quarry's magic, too. As for me, I'm waiting for the right moment to leave everyone and swim over to my boulder.

Marco's reached us. "Did Jolie tell you what a great model she is?" he asks. "I think her face is just what I've needed for my photos here. She can look young, yet old; playful, yet serious; innocent, yet wise—"

"So you figured out how smart she is," Mom interrupts him to say.

I don't want to fool him. "Mom's wrong. I'm not that smart. I just study a lot."

"She's being modest. Did you tell him that you were almost the salutatorian at your junior high school?" Mom says, as she starts running her hand over my wet hair.

I shake off her hand. "*Almost* doesn't count."

"It does to me," Marco says with a laugh.

"To me, too," Mom says.

"To me, three!" Harry pipes up.

We're all laughing now, including me, even though I know I'm about to hear it again, the story Mom loves telling.

"What happened, Marco, is that Jolie's vice principal, Dr. Fleishman, called her into his office to congratulate her on being the ninth grade salutatorian. That honor goes to the girl with the highest grades in her junior high graduating class. Right, Jojo?"

I nod. She goes on.

"He told her to write a speech that night for graduation, and they'd go over it in the morning. And she told *him* that her best friend, Elyse, had higher grades than her.

Chapter 5 - The Skinny One

So then he said that his office couldn't possibly make a mistake. Right, Jojo?"

I nod again. Must she continue?

"He acted like she was trying to weasel her way out of writing a speech. Can you imagine!" Mom says, shaking her head.

"Really!" Marco looks surprised that someone would think I'd lie.

Dad's the exact opposite. Sometimes I wonder why I bother being honest if he never believes me.

"That night Jolie wrote a speech, like he told her to, and the next morning Dr. Fleishman called her into his office, right?"

"Right again," I mumble.

"And he said it turned out that his office actually *had* made a mistake."

"That must have made you feel great," Marco says, like he knows it did not.

I nod and turn away. At least Mom can't tell him the rest, because I never told her: how I told Dr. Fleishman, "See, I was right," in a normal, sane voice, and a second later, started sobbing. I had to stay in his office all morning, with my crumpled speech in my lap because I couldn't stop crying. I kept thinking how unfair life is. No matter how much I study, I'm screwed. I don't have parents like Elyse, who want her to go to college like they did, who read good books and discuss them with her and listen to what she says.

Quarry Face

She's got all the luck, while I've got a father who makes fun of people who are educated and jumps down my throat like everything I think is wrong and a mom who never finished high school and only reads movie magazines and romance novels. Oh, I know she means well and I love her, but I wish I had someone at home I could talk to, like Elyse does.

On graduation day, her parents surprised her with a trip to Paris. A whole month there, as a reward for her hard work! They actually rented an apartment! My parents surprised me, too. They said they were separating. Mom said they hadn't wanted to break the news until I got done with finals and my graduation ceremony. When I started crying, Mom probably thought I was feeling bad for her, but really I cried because I knew that from then on, whenever I thought about my junior high graduation, I'd remember my parents breaking up. Couldn't they have picked another day? Okay, not my birthday or a holiday or anybody else's birthday I celebrate. But there are plenty of other days to choose from.

I turn back, about to tell Marco he's right, that I felt lousy. Instead I say, "Marco, turn around."

"Hi, mates," he says when he does.

∼

The two boys are floating next to Marco on what looks like a raft made from wooden planks. They're steering with long branches, reminding me of *Huckleberry Finn*.

"Hi," The Skinny One says after swerving to avoid hitting us. The second boy, on the far end of the raft, grunts. He's wearing the kind of sunglasses I hate because

Chapter 5 - The Skinny One

you see your own reflection in them, not the other person's eyes.

"Neat raft," Marco says.

"Thanks. Say, you guys don't own this place, do you?" The Skinny One asks.

Looks shouldn't matter. But I think he's cute, with his straight, light brown hair flopping over his forehead and an expression like he finds everything amusing. He reminds me of the drummer, Ringo Starr, who's the most adorable member of the Beatles, except he's chunkier than The Skinny One.

"I thought *you* guys were the owners!" Marco says.

"Yeah, right," The Skinny One says and both boys chuckle. Then, pushing the hair off his forehead, The Skinny One asks us all, "You ever see the frogs?"

I need a new bathing suit.

Harry and I nod.

"They're a riot! But she hasn't seen them yet," Marco points to Mom. "She's in for a treat."

"Yeah, nothing beats the first time," The Skinny One says.

His friend cracks up laughing. The Skinny One looks ready to laugh, too, but then the other guy grunts and says, "Ready to shove off, King?"

"Just hold your horses, Dog Breath," The Skinny One replies.

Harry giggles.

"So, has anyone ever tried to kick you boys out of here?"

"No ma'am," The Skinny One answers Mom. "My older brother, Allen, who used to swim here all the time, said that whoever owns this place probably forgot it even exists."

"Hey, we gotta go," says the other boy. Without waiting for a response, he stands up and starts pushing off with his stick.

The Skinny One reaches for his own stick. As the raft starts drifting away, he points it from me to Harry and calls out, "You two should come to The Video Palace. You'll like it, especially you, kid. They've got the latest video games."

"Really!" Harry says and looks at Mom and me with clasped hands.

I walked by The Video Palace with Harry last week. It's in Carmel Plaza, near the mini-department store Mom works at. Harry tried getting me to go in, but a bunch of kids my age were leaving, joking around. I distracted him with a visit to Putnam Pets.

The Skinny One nods at Harry, then waves with just one finger of his right hand. Cute. I wave back, but with my whole left hand. I wonder if The Skinny One knows anything about my boulder.

Suddenly, the sky darkens.

Chapter 5 - The Skinny One

Boom! *Boom!*

"Uh oh. Might just be a sun shower, but let's not take any chances," Marco says. And with that, he starts pulling Harry's float towards the clearing.

The sky's rapidly getting darker. Mom's turning our float so we can follow Marco and Harry back to shore.

The rain's pounding on the Volvo's roof and all of us are wet by the time Marco starts driving away. I don't see the boys out the back window. I hope they're okay, not that I even know their names. Skinny and Grumpy? So, is The Skinny One really part of my story? That thought had been strong, as if it had to be true.

"You know, too much thinking can be a dangerous thing," Marco says.

He's watching me in his rearview mirror.

"How come?" Harry asks, while he fidgets with the floats squished up on our laps. We ran for cover too fast to deflate them.

"Never mind," Marco replies.

He and Mom laugh.

Harry makes a face. I don't blame him. I hate when adults act like they know everything. They don't. Nobody does.

Quarry Face

"Hey, I nearly forgot. Fran, can you open up my glove compartment. There's a book in there for Jolie."

"Really?" I say. That's a surprise.

Mom pulls out a paperback, and when Marco nods, she hands it over.

"Mira said you should read it," Marco says.

"Mirror? Like you see your reflection in?" I ask.

"Her name's spelled M-i-r-a. She's my—well— maybe she's still my girlfriend."

"Ohhhh," Mom says, and pats Marco on the arm.

That's Mom! She loves stories with happy endings. Marco's shrugging like a shy little boy. He and Mom look so cute together. But what is this book? Its blue front cover has a drawing of a flying saucer hovering over a city and the words ARTHUR C. CLARKE, CHILDHOOD'S END in the middle of the cover. At the top, in yellow type, it reads *Science Fiction's Big Bestseller By the Author of* **2001 A Space Odyssey.** *Over 1,000,000 copies in print.*

"Over a million copies in print and I've never heard of it," I say. "See, I told you I'm not smart. But why does your friend, Mira, think I should read it? She doesn't know me from Adam."

"The last time we talked on the phone, I told her you had found your way to her favorite spot in the quarry, and she said to give you her copy of *Childhood's End*."

"Her favorite spot? You mean that rock I sat on?"

Chapter 5 - The Skinny One

Marco nods.

"Does she live near here? Can I meet her?"

"Let's not bother Marco with a lot of personal questions," Mom tells me.

"That's okay. No, she doesn't live near here. These days she's traveling, more than living in any one spot…"

He stops speaking. Mom turns to me with a look that emphasizes what she's said. I lean back in my seat, and while Harry looks over my shoulder, I flip through the first few pages of *Childhood's End*. It was published in 1953 and this is its 39th printing. It might be interesting. But what I'd really like, more than a science fiction bestseller, and even more than writing a good poem, would be someone to talk to—to really talk to—someone to be completely honest with.

In the meantime, I guess I should be glad I've got my journal to keep. Tonight, I'll write about seeing The Skinny One again, and his suggestion that we visit The Video Palace. Maybe we will.

Chapter 6
The Question

> The truth is a gift
> For sharing with care
> By those moving on,
> The future their sphere.
>   Jolie Rich
>   Carmel, New York

"C'mon, get across there, get across."

The Skinny One said that. He's playing Froggers, which in Brooklyn only little kids play. It's a video game where you try to get your frogs across the road without them getting squashed by all kinds of vehicles. Harry, who ran ahead of me as soon as we entered The Video Palace, is reaching over to touch The Skinny One's arm. Meanwhile, all these noises and flashing lights are everywhere you turn. Harry must love it.

"Holy shit, did you see that?" The Skinny One suddenly yells, while he bangs on the game's glass top.

His friends all laugh.

Harry laughs, too.

Chapter 6 - The Question

"Hey, mind your tongue, young man," shouts a short, roly-poly man walking by, jingling change in his apron pocket.

"Oh, so sorry, so sorry," The Skinny One bows deeply.

His friends laugh harder. The four of them are probably around my age, and they're still laughing when Harry finally taps The Skinny One on his arm. He looks at my brother and smiles. Then he looks over at me as I approach.

"The quarry, remember?" I say.

"I do, except now you've got clothes on."

His friends laugh more.

"I was wearing a bathing suit," I explain.

"Sure you were," The Skinny One says.

More laughter. This is a very giggly group.

"So, you didn't just move here, did you?" The Skinny One asks.

"We're house-sitting for our aunt on Stoneleigh Avenue—"

"We come from Brooklyn!" Harry interrupts.

"Brooklyn! Where's that?" It's Grumpy. I recognize his voice. He looks better without sunglasses.

"Don't let us get to you. We're like this with everyone," The Skinny One says after the laughter subsides. "Let me introduce you. That's Bobby, the sourpuss you met the other day. This is Dominick and Carrie. And that's Andi, she's our token female redhead. Every group needs one."

Andi pretends to give The Skinny One a karate kick.

"Yeah, but what's *your* name?" Harry asks, like he caught The Skinny One trying to get away with something.

"I knew I forgot someone. I'm Erik, spelled with a k. And who are you?"

"I'm Harry!"

"I'm his sister, Jolie," I say. "Hi, everyone."

Erik's smile grows as his friends say hi. He looks from me to them. Then, looking back at me, he asks, "So, your folks around much during the day?"

"Right to the point, aren't you, King?" Carrie says. She's blonde and wearing a low-cut top, just like my cousin Martha likes.

"We better go. Nice meeting you guys." Without waiting for a reply, I swing Harry around and point him towards the exit.

"I didn't get to play even one game," Harry says, when we're back outside. He's looking at his wristwatch. "And we weren't even there ten minutes."

The day's hot and sticky.

"I'm sorry. The noise made me bonkers," I fib, because I don't want to tell him what I really think. He's too young

Chapter 6 - The Question

to know how people are. "Hey, let's walk over to Angela's Deli. Maybe they'll have something new for us to sample."

"Bonkers!" Harry repeats, as he picks up the pace.

∽

Angela's Italian Deli comes through again. The owners always have cheese for us to sample, although they must know by now that we won't buy more than an Italian bread if Mom's not with us. By the time we're ready to leave, Harry's his usual happy self.

As we walk outside, we see Erik leaning against Angela's front window, smoking.

"Hi! We got to try some cheese that tastes like soap," Harry tells him.

"It was Brie," I explain, pronouncing it how Marco taught us to last night. Mom said she might have tasted it once before. I never did. We had it while Marco showed us his slides from France. Harry's right, Brie tastes like soap.

Erik flicks away some ashes from his cigarette. "You ran off so fast, like maybe we upset you."

"We had to get this." I hold up a long, crusty Italian bread in a white paper bag. Then I lower my voice and cup my hand to one side of my mouth. "I thought you were only interested in us because we might have an empty house for you guys to hang out in."

"That's wacky," Erik says and shakes his head.

Harry giggles, "Wacky! Wacky."

I can't help smiling. Harry has that effect on me. And wacky is a pretty funny word.

Erik's smiling back at me. He takes a few more drags. "You walking this way? I'm going to work."

Harry's tugging at my arm. I know where he wants to go. I nod.

"Just stay in sight," I yell as he runs ahead. Erik and I continue on. "So, where do you work?"

"I'm a hamburger slinger at McDonald's, but maybe not for much longer," Erik says with a chuckle.

"How come?"

McDonalds! I see its golden arches whenever I take a shower. In fact, this morning, while the hot water was pouring over me to get all my conditioner out, I was laughing to myself how I see those arches while Elyse wrote, in the letter I opened this morning but may not answer, that the Eiffel Tower looks 'magnifique' from her bedroom. *Magnifique!*

"My manager says I clown around too much. But who can take serving fast food seriously?"

"Probably someone with a family of ten to support," I say.

"How old are you, forty?"

"I had a *magnifique* plastic surgeon, darling. I simply must give you his name. Simply *magnifique!*"

Chapter 6 - The Question

Erik looks totally puzzled.

"I didn't *really* have plastic surgery. It's something a character said in a movie called *Breakfast At Tiffanys*. Anyway, I'm not forty."

"No, I know you're not," Erik says, crushing his cigarette beneath his sneaker. He takes a pack from his back pocket and holds it out to me.

"I don't smoke."

"You're smart."

"I know. So, why do you smoke?"

"Guess I'm not so smart."

"I guess not."

"Look, how old are you really? Sixteen?" Erik taps out a cigarette.

"You're warm." I'm surprised. Most people say I look young for my age, which I usually hate. Mom and Aunt Tish say I'll be glad when I get older if people still tell me that.

"Okay, you're seventeen."

"Two down," I reply.

"Not fifteen!"

"What about you?" I ask as we pass a group of people who are dancing around, chanting. They're all wearing

Quarry Face

embroidered white robes. The men are completely bald, and the women have very long hair. They're selling candles and incense and behind them there's a huge poster of an Asian-looking man.

"They're followers of Joy Star," Erik says with a frown. He looks back at them. "Weird cult. Don't know why they're allowed around here, but they are."

"Freedom of speech, I guess," I tell him. "I saw a news report about them on TV. They think Joy Star is God! The reporter said that if you talk to them long enough, they try to brainwash you into joining them."

"Yeah, I know," Erik says. He looks like he's about to add more, but just then we reach Harry, who's singing while tapping on the window of Putnam Pets.

I pull his hand away from the glass because the salesman inside is throwing him glares. The three kittens Harry's watching look like fluffy fur balls. With his hands behind him, Harry continues his rendition of "How much is that kitty in the window?"

"Okay, now it's your turn to guess my age," Erik says.

"I'm lousy at guessing games."

"C'mon, fair's fair."

He's lighting up again. When he's done, I stare at his face. He's got nice, sensitive eyes and a pointy nose. A guy in one of Mom's romance novels had lips the writer described as 'sensual.' Erik's are like that, full and soft. This is stupid. "Okay, you're seventeen."

Chapter 6 - The Question

"Did you see my learner's permit?"

"I'm right? Maybe I should buy a lottery ticket."

Erik gives me another puzzled look, then checks his wristwatch. "I better split so I don't get docked for being late. But listen, you should drop by The Palace some night," he says, lowering his voice, "and without the kid. That's where the action is. Well, whatever action there is around here."

"My mom probably won't let me go alone, but maybe when my cousin comes up next weekend. She's sixteen and a half."

"Is she cute?"

"Looks shouldn't matter, but if you must know, yes, Martha's cute. Right, Harry?"

Harry shrugs.

"Okay, so what if I ask you out on a double date? You and your cousin, and me and a friend of mine. Not one of the loonies back there."

"But you don't even know me."

"And you don't know me, so we're even. Look, I don't make *dates*," he says, like the very word amuses him. "But I figure any girl with a half-eaten apple on her chest has got to be worth knowing. Your name's not Eve, is it?

Eve? Chest? Oh, he means the apple on my *I Love The Big Apple* t-shirt. He must be thinking of Eve from The Garden of Eden. She gave Adam an apple, which stood

53

for knowledge, not that I understand what's wrong with knowing as much as possible.

"Why, are you Adam?"

"As a matter of fact, yes."

"You said your name's Erik."

"Erik Butler Adams."

"You're a butler!" Harry squeals.

"At your service," Erik bows. "So what's your full name? Jolie what?"

"Jolie Eve."

"Eve!" Erik's eyes widen.

"Only kidding. I'm Jolie Rich. No middle name." He looks like he really believed me.

"Rich? You putting me on again?" Erik says.

"Daddy says we're the poorest Riches in the world," Harry tells him.

That's one of our father's biggest jokes, not that I find it even approaches being funny. Harry's tugging on my arm. Kids under twelve can't enter Putnam's Pets unchaperoned.

"The kid's getting antsy. Anyway, I better split," Erik says. He pulls out a matchbook and a stubby pencil from his pants pocket. "Here. Write down your phone number. I'll call to set a time and get your address. I'm not scheduled

Chapter 6 - The Question

for Saturday night, so we can do something then." He stops and shakes his head. "I can't believe I'm asking you out."

And I can't believe I'm accepting. "But my mom might not let me—"

Before I finish, Erik says, "It's worth a shot."

When I hand everything back, he reads my aunt's phone number aloud as if he's reciting it for the kittens. Harry finds that hilarious. And after I nod that he got it right, Erik says he'll call Thursday night. I nod again, though I won't hold my breath. Dad said lots of things he didn't mean. And what if, just saying, Erik's secretly competing with his friends to see who can get the most girls' phone numbers on matchbook covers this summer? Anyway, do I really want to go *on a date* with him? Martha says I'll love dating once I start, but I've got my doubts.

He's running now, and waving with just one finger, like he did in the quarry. Has he ever been on my rock? Does he know anything about it?

"Why are you waving? He can't see you," Harry says as he tugs at my arm.

I didn't realize I was waving.

That does it. As soon as we get back to the cottage, I'll phone Martha and ask her to help me figure out how to get Mom to say yes to Erik Butler Adams becoming my first real date.

Chapter 7
Who *Are* You?

> Love's in the air,
> And the air smells divine.
> How sweet to be young,
> With decades to mine.
> Jolie Rich
> Carmel, New York

"Hey, Louie, thanks!" Erik calls out, as his friend heads back to Peking Palace's front counter, where he's working the cash register tonight. Louie is the owner's son and he just left us with a big dish of pistachio ice cream to share. He also brought us fortune cookies and played a game with them. He cracked them all open, put them in the middle of the table, then had us draw numbers for the order in which we got to choose which fortune we wanted. Erik went first and picked "Choose adventure over comfort." Martha's date Jimmy went next, selecting "You are one of those who will go places in life." Third to pick, Martha chose "A refreshing change is in your future." I had no other choice but to take "You will make a name for yourself." Not that I believe in fortune cookies any more than in Aunt Tish's horoscopes.

Chapter 7 - Who Are You?

"Louie always hooks me up with free ice cream," Erik says, turning back to the rest of us. "But it works both ways. I give him free cones at McDonalds when nobody's looking."

"Isn't that illegal?" I blurt out, before I can stop my words. I hate sounding so goody goody.

"Everything's against the law," Erik laughs. "Laws are meant to be broken."

"He gives me free cones, too," adds Jimmy, who's got more freckles than anyone I've ever seen.

I guess they go with his red hair. Martha once told me that redheaded guys give her the creeps. I probably reminded her that looks shouldn't matter. But I didn't think to ask Erik the color of his friend's hair. Do you ask stuff like that when you double date?

"And what do you give him?" Martha asks Jimmy.

She glances across the table at me and winks, like she often does when she's having a good time. Tonight, she's winking so much, she's nearly blinking. I don't think she's getting the creeps. Maybe it'll all be okay.

Jimmy whips out a small card holder from his shirt pocket. Handing Martha and me each a card from it, he says, "I give his mom a big discount on antiques."

I read my card aloud. "Poorboy Antiques/James O'Malley Proprietor/Free Lemonade Just For Looking." Then I stare at Jimmy.

"But you're a senior in high school like Erik. How do you find time to run a business? Is this a joke?"

Erik laughs. "No joke. He collects stuff from yard and rummage sales on Saturdays, then sells them in his parents' barn on Sundays. Don't you, Jimbo?"

Jimmy nods with a silly face, like he's one of the Three Stooges. He's a bit of a character. But then, I suppose, so am I.

"So, what's next?" Martha asks, licking the last remains of pistachio ice cream from her spoon.

"It's too late for a movie, so let's drive to where we get the best view of the valley," Erik says, brushing the hair from his eyes.

"Sure, that sounds *super!*" Martha says with a giggle. "Let's go."

I flash her a pointed look.

"Don't worry, you'll like it. I promise," Erik says, as if he's reading my mind.

But, of course, he's not really. And I'm not about to admit that Mom warned us not to let our dates take us somewhere secluded. I should have expected trouble when Martha changed into a see-through blouse for tonight. She was not thrilled about wearing my t-shirt over it. I blamed Mom, said she'd have conniptions—but it was my doing.

Still, Martha seems happy now. In fact, all of Peking Palace's customers seem happy, everyone's laughing and eating and talking. Why can't I be like them?

Chapter 7 - Who Are You?

Why must I keep worrying about what's coming next? And that I won't remember everything for my journal? I don't mean what I'm seeing—the walls with their murals of bright red Chinese dragons, the plates decorated with blue peacocks, our cracked teapot, the food we shared, or the chopsticks that Jimmy knew how to use best. (His grandpa took him along on a business trip to Hong Kong three years ago.) What I'm obsessed with are conversations. Tonight's are especially important, since I'll never have a second first date. This is it.

I wish I knew Erik well enough to ask him to take us to the quarry. But Mom would kill me if we went there tonight. He's starting to get up. Martha and Jimmy are, too. I check my watch. How long do dates usually last?

∽

"So, do you like driving a Chevy Citation?" Martha asks as she and Jimmy climb into the back seat. "It's a pretty fancy car. Very cushiony back here."

"It was my old man's," Erik replies, as he opens the passenger door for me.

Something in his tone makes me think we shouldn't ask more questions. I throw Martha a look. She nods. And soon we're headed up a hill in the dark. I'm glad there's a full moon, but still, I don't feel at ease.

"You don't say much, do you?" Erik says.

It's more a statement than a question.

"I guess not."

"See if you can find us a good station," he says next, nodding at the radio.

I don't blame him. I bet he'd rather be with Martha, who's giggling with Jimmy behind us. Nothing, absolutely nothing, bothers her.

"Leave it," Erik says when I come to a station playing "Penny Lane."

"I love the Beatles," I tell him.

"Me too. I hope there's a good rock station at Allegheny. Otherwise, I'll really be pissed."

At Peking Palace he mentioned he'd be a freshman at Allegheny College in Meadville, Pennsylvania, this fall.

"Why Allegheny? I've never heard of it before," I say.

"It's the only college that'll take him," Jimmy shouts over the music.

He and Martha howl with laughter.

"Yeah, I'm a lazy son of a bitch," Erik says, then mumbles, "I wouldn't be going to college at all if my mom didn't insist we use some of my old man's life insurance money on it. She says he won't rest in peace until I graduate."

"Your father died?" I ask.

"Six months ago. Heart attack. The doctors said he had a bad heart that nobody knew about."

Chapter 7 - Who Are You?

"He was a good guy, your dad," Jimmy says, leaning on the back of my seat. "Everyone liked him."

"I'm sorry he died," I say. I mean it. Death sounds so final, no chance to talk to each other ever again. Poor Erik.

"Well, don't be. Getting excused from this rathole is a blessing."

Before I can ask Erik why he thinks something so depressing, the deejay announces we're in the first hour of an all-night tribute to the Beatles, and Erik screeches to a stop.

"We're here, kiddos," he says and turns off the headlights.

"What a view!" Martha yells, opening her back door.

"My compliments to God," shouts Jimmy, practically tumbling out after her.

"You coming?" Erik asks, after getting out his side.

Jimmy and Martha are giggling as they disappear behind some trees. Thanks a lot, Martha. It's not cold out, but I wrap my cardigan over my shoulders before slamming my door shut.

"Check that out," Erik says, coming up beside me.

He's pointing to a house on a hilltop that's silhouetted against the full moon. He's left the radio on, and right now "Get Back" is playing with the lyrics "Get back, Jojo, back to where you once belonged." I like it because it's got my nickname. Marco played the same song when he showed us slides from our first visit to the quarry. But he didn't have any shots of my rock, and Harry wanted more slides of frogs. Marco promised his next slide show would have both. I must admit, however, that he made me look really good. I usually hate seeing photos of myself, but not his.

Erik's still pointing to the house, like he's waiting for my response.

And now that I'm giving the house my full attention, its silhouette looks like a huge doorway that goes through the moon to somewhere much farther away. I'm not sure I can explain to Erik what I see, but I'll give it a try.

"The shape of that house is amazing. It looks like you can walk right through it, like it's an entrance to the rest of the Solar System, or the universe, or maybe even to another dimension. Do you see what I mean?"

"You see that?" Erik says, moving his head around and squinting. "Actually, it's a deserted mansion on Solomon Hill. It's got twenty-four bedrooms. My old man used to joke about buying it someday when his ship came in. I'd tell him, 'Dad, your only ship is hardship.'"

His voice trails off. He's lighting a cigarette.

This feels like the right time. Seeing that house makes this feel like the right place, too. While leaning against the side of his car, I ask, "Erik? When you were at the quarry, did you ever sit on a very smooth boulder that's got a flower, a big white flower, growing on it?"

"I've sat on a lot of boulders in the quarry. I'm not sure. Why?"

Chapter 7 - Who Are You?

"Oh, just curious." I think he'd know exactly which one I meant if he'd had an experience like mine. He's staring at that mansion. Or maybe he's staring at the moon.

"You ever think about living on the moon someday?" I ask. "Or on Mars?"

"What are you, a space cadet?" Erik asks with a laugh.

"My Aunt Tish calls me that. She says it's in my chart. Don't laugh. That's what she says, not that I believe in astrology."

"Me either," Erik replies, then laughs again. "But what's your sign?"

"You first. What are you?"

"Virgo. Very down to earth," he says, moving closer to me.

There's tobacco on his breath, and I think that's baby shampoo in his hair. His hip brushes against mine.

"I'm a Gemini," I say as I move away from him. "Aunt Tish says lots of writers are Geminis, if you believe that kind of stuff."

"I'm not going to hurt you," Erik says, his voice dropping.

"I know." Maybe arranged marriages are the way to go.

"You're a strange girl, you know. So, let me tell you something, strange girl. One day before we met in the quarry, Jimbo and me were riding our bikes and we saw you down there. And I told him, 'I've got to meet her.' Really. Don't ask me why. I just did," Erik says, shaking his head.

"Maybe you're psychic." I'm certainly not going to say what I thought when I first saw *him*. Maybe we're both bonkers.

"Psychic? Hey, maybe I am," Erik says. "Maybe you are, too."

"I doubt it. I've tried talking to birds with telepathy. Nothing happens."

I can't believe I just told him that.

"Birds? Why not humans?" he asks, like I'm not a total weirdo.

"Because of something strange that happened to me once." Me and my big mouth. I'm boxing myself into a corner.

"Tell me what it was or I'll tickle it out of you," Erik says.

"Nowhere Man" is playing. I wish I could write songs, but only happy ones. Erik sounds so cute and he looks like he's really curious. "Promise you won't laugh?"

"Scout's honor."

"And you won't think I'm crazy?"

"I already do."

Chapter 7 - Who Are You?

I've never told anyone what happened, not Elyse, not Martha—nobody. So why tell Erik? I just feel like I should. "It happened in third grade. My teacher, this nice lady named Mrs. Richardson, was walking to the back of the classroom to open a window. And I heard fire engines coming down the block and I thought to myself, 'When they pass under our window, Mrs. Richardson will fall.'"

"Did you hate her?"

"Not at all. But I used to try to will things to happen, I guess to test myself."

"And could you?" Erik's lighting another cigarette.

Here comes the tough part. "Just as the fire engines passed under our window, Mrs. Richardson fell. It was horrible. She couldn't get up. She sent the class vice president for a nurse, and she told the class president to keep order in the classroom. Luckily, she only got bruises. She retired the next year."

"I better not get you mad at me."

"Don't worry. It had to be a coincidence. But since then, I don't try psychic stuff on humans." I pause, trying to gauge Erik's reaction. "You're giving me a weird look. You do think I'm crazy. See?"

"No, I'm glad you told me."

I'm sure I said too much. I was going to ask him if he'd read *Childhood's End,* but not after the look he just shot me. Oh, why did I have to open my big mouth? I'd have loved to talk to him about how these aliens in it, called Overlords, come to Earth and start making it a better place. He'd probably just say, "It figures you'd like stuff like that." The Overlords put an end to wars and poverty and inequality, but not everyone trusts them, because they're not saying why they're here. I'm just guessing their reasons, but whatever they are, *Childhood's End* is the best book I've ever read.

Last night I got up to the part where they finally reveal what they look like. Before that they spoke to the human being they used as their messenger without his seeing them. Now they've revealed themselves to everybody, and it turns out they look like ancient demons, with horns and tails. I thought of Grandfatherly Figure. He's the exact opposite.

Erik hasn't interrupted my thoughts. He's silently staring at that entranceway I fantasized. He's probably thinking of it as a solid brick mansion.

"Do you ever think there might be people on other planets to communicate with?" I ask, looking where Erik's looking. "I hope there are."

"Why would you want that?" he asks. "That's just asking for trouble. They might make us slaves, or kill us for the planet if they know we exist. We've got enough problems with our own people killing each other."

"That's pessimistic," I say.

"Is it? I think it's more realistic," he says, and before I can come up with a good reply, he's cupping his hands around his mouth and yelling, "Jimbo! Martha! Get your butts here on the double or you're walking home." He turns to me. "Don't worry, Princess. I'll get you home way before curfew."

Chapter 7 - Who Are You?

Princess? The word makes me grin. "If I'm a princess, does that make you a prince?"

Without a word, Erik holds open my car door. Just as I get in, John Lennon is singing, "You may say that I'm a dreamer, but I'm not the only one. Someday I hope you'll join us, and the world can live as one."

Too bad he was murdered. I love this song, and lots more of Lennon's.

Erik doesn't say a peep all the while he's getting seated behind the wheel, and slamming his door. Then, grinning, he repeats my question, "Does that make me a prince, you want to know? "He pauses like a comedian might, then concludes, "Me? I ain't nothin' but a bullfrog."

∽

"So, did he ask you out again?" Martha whispers.

She's punching the pillow I gave her to use with the sleeping bag she's spread out on the floor next to my bed.

"He said we'll probably see each other in the quarry," I reply. I'm sure he was just being nice.

I yawn and turn off my lamp. I'll try to get up very early tomorrow, so I can write about tonight before Martha wakes up.

"You know what Jimmy said? The next time I visit, he'll give me one of his old blue glass bottles! Other girls get diamonds, and Mercedes, and—

"—trips to Paris…"

"Right, and trips to Paris, but what do I get? An old bottle!"

"But did you like him, Mart?"

"He was fun for a night, but too far out for me. He kept asking crazy questions, like do I think God's real and will Jesus be returning any time soon. I said, 'How the hell should I know! I'm Jewish.'" Martha tells me, muffling her laughter. Then she whispers, "Just one thing, Jo. Watch out for Erik. Guys like him are dangerous."

"Dangerous? How do you mean? Like a vampire or a serial killer?"

"Don't play dumb. You know what I mean. They think they're God's gift to women and girls fall for them all the time, which they take advantage of. I just don't want you hurt."

"I doubt if you have to worry. Erik will probably never call again. I acted like an idiot! Actually, I acted natural. That's the problem. I'm not made for dating."

"You have to give yourself a chance. Dating can be fun. Besides, how can you find someone to marry if you don't date him first? Hey, can you imagine! Jimmy wants to give me a bottle? I should ask him for one with a genie in it."

After Martha's last few slurred words and a few laughs, nothing more comes out of her mouth but snores. It's amazing how my skinny, sexy cousin can produce such loud foghorns. I turn towards the wall with my pillow over my head. I shut my eyes. The sheet feels cool and comfy. And I'm very tired.

Chapter 7 - Who Are You?

But I'm not falling asleep.

Instead, I'm hearing the conversations I'll write in my journal tomorrow: those at Peking Palace and in the car and on the hill, like from when we looked at the house on Solomon Hill and, oh, wait a second. I'm taking a detour. Now I'm on the hill above the quarry, and I can see tadpoles swimming near the surface, their tails intertwined to form a gigantic circle. They're calling up to me, those tadpoles, except no words are said out loud. Still, I know they're telling me, *Come join us and we'll play on Earth's last childhood's day.*

The next thing I know, it's morning.

Chapter 8
Why Not Erik?

> Some will see between the lines
> And embrace.
> Others will see nothing.
> No disgrace.
> Jolie Rich
> Carmel, New York

I'm standing on the stoop, trying not to think of Erik, when there he is, walking his bike towards me. This I did not expect. I feel like I'm staring at him with a stupid look on my face as he stops near me and holds out something.

"Here, I brought you a present," he says.

"It's fuzzy. Thank you," I say, taking the small, green stuffed animal from him. It's a frog. Why's he here? He's got to hate me. Maybe he lost something Saturday night.

"I saw it in a gift shop when I was buying a birthday card for my brother, and I thought you might like it."

"Really?" I can feel myself smiling a big smile in response to the sheepish look on his face. Is this the same

Chapter 8 - Why Not Erik?

Erik who was with me on Solomon Hill? Why's he here now?

"Did you—"

Before I can finish, Marco and Harry are running up behind him, and Marco's saying, "I remember you. From the quarry? Hi. I'm Marco."

"Erik."

"And you know me. I'm Harry," says my brother. He looks happy that I let him go over to Marco's earlier. Actually, I was glad I could do that, so I got to write some.

"We just came to get Jolie for the quarry. Hey, want to come along?" Marco asks.

Erik nods.

Wait a minute. This is weird, going to the quarry with Erik. All week long, I swatted away every thought of him, and now I'm getting goose bumps again, like on the hilltop. But even if I'm wrong about him hating me, I planned to float off on my own today and go you-know-where, because Marco could watch Harry. This changes everything.

Maybe Erik will want to hang out with the guys.

～

"So, any idea what you'll major in?" Marco's asking Erik now, as we're on our way to the quarry. He's already asked a bunch of questions about Allegheny College.

"Getting out," Erik says. "That's my major."

"He doesn't mean it, Harry. He's just joking. Once he starts college, he'll love it, won't you, Erik?" I quickly say, but with a smile.

Erik shrugs at me with a crazy expression that makes my brother giggle, and all of a sudden it comes back to me, my thinking Erik's part of my story.

I turn towards the front and stare straight ahead. Wow. I should remember to write down that thought in my journal. Plus my latest attempt to talk to a bird, which took place right before Erik showed up.

#65. Negative.

It's hard figuring out whether to read or write at night because I've got so little energy left when I finally have time to myself. I feel like I'll go nuts if I don't write, even if it's just a few rhymed sentences, but there's also *Childhood's End* to read. It's dated in some details, so you know it's fiction, but it's so compelling, if that's the right word. I love it so much. I'm up to the part now where the Overlords have been on Earth for a generation and people are getting used to them, and a woman named Jeanne is about to give birth to a child who means something special to the Overlords, although I don't know what. And that's not all. There's a guy plotting to stow away on one of the Overlords' supply ships so he can go to their home planet and see what it's like, and he's getting closer and closer to his goal.

I know. It sounds like I'm a really slow reader, but that's because I feel like I want to savor every word. I don't want the book to end. I'm so glad Marco's friend said I should read it.

∼

Chapter 8 - Why Not Erik?

At the gate, Erik lifts one side on his own, which means Harry and I lift the other, and Marco can drive through without getting out of his car. Like always, I hate, hate, *hate* sneaking past a KEEP OUT sign, but only until we're at the top of the hill and I can breathe in the quarry air. Then, screw the sign! I'm back. And in just a little while we'll be down the hill, in the water, and I'll be headed… home again. Or else, to where I'll know I've been fantasizing everything.

I can't let anything stop me. Nothing. That includes Erik.

At our spot, he offers to help Marco inflate the floats.

"Me and my mate, Harry, have everything under control," Marco tells him.

Harry beams like a miniature sun! I love that Marco!

"I was planning to go swimming anyway," Erik says, wiggling out of his tan shorts. He's got his swim trunks on.

He pulls off his tan t-shirt and lets it drop to the ground.

"Can you read that?" I ask, pointing to the writing on the shirt next to a silkscreened photo of the Great Wall of China. It looks like it's in Chinese characters.

"It means *I Climbed The Great Wall of China*," Erik replies.

"But you didn't real—"

"I'll get my raft and be right back," Erik says before I'm done.

Quarry Face

Then he's diving into the water and swimming away.

Just as well. He doesn't have to see me take off my t-shirt, 'cause I feel a bit weird wearing a new bathing suit. Of course, Martha says it looks just like my old one, except it's blue. She kept wanting me to try on bikinis when we went shopping, but I kept reminding her I'm not a bikini person. Besides, this suit makes my hips look smaller than bikinis do. Martha says my big hips are all in my mind. I disagree. I'm built like Mom. Even if I wasn't, I'm a lot more shy than my cousin. Sometimes I wish I were more like Martha. Sometimes I wish Martha were more like me. A lot of times I wish I didn't wish.

Erik's reached the shore. He steadies the raft with his stick, then puts one foot on the step, and leans toward me.

"Take my hand," he says.

"You sure about this?" I say with a smile.

"Don't worry, I won't let you fall, Princess," Erik replies.

His hand's cold and wet, and the raft wobbles when I jump over, and what did he just say?

"You called me 'princess' again," I say as I seat myself, legs crossed.

"Yeah, you look like a princess to me today," he says with a laugh.

It's a different kind of laugh than on our date. It's almost, oh, I don't know, tender, maybe.

Chapter 8 - Why Not Erik?

"So, where to, Princess? Wait, let me guess." He puts one palm on his forehead and shuts his eyes, like a swami I once saw on television. "You want to go to—yes, I see it all—that rock with the antisocial flower, right?"

"Not antisocial, but yes!" I say, surprised he remembered. I wasn't sure what to do about him, but now I am. Okay, so we'll go to my boulder together.

I point the way, but when we're close enough to touch it, something doesn't seem right. "It needs a name. I know. Let's call it Sunwake."

"Sunwake? How come?" Erik asks, while he grabs on to the boulder and jumps over.

I don't answer until he's pulled me over, tied up his raft, and sat down on the other side of the flower from me. "Sunwake's what came to me. Like 'princess' came to you. Do you ever wonder where thoughts come from?"

"Where thoughts come from? What do you mean?" Erik repeats, like he finds my question silly. He's expecting me to reply.

Sorry. I can't wait another second. I close my eyes. I focus on the white flower, the image of it in my mind. Got to act quickly, because I'm not alone. I'm all set to mentally shape a beam of light on which to send a message.

You're back! Oh, goody!

It's Erma! She's wearing a flowing gown like before, only this time it looks more beautiful than I remember. I'd love a gown like that, although it looks perfect on her. It's white, yet I could swear I see a rainbow of colors, as if it's changing as I watch. And we're in some kind of tannish space again, with *nice* gray blobs all around us, and I'm feeling I'm where I belong, like everything I'll see again when I open my eyes is a dream while this is real. The quarry gives me confidence, but this is home. Confirmation, check!

This time you've got to tell me where I am, I say in my head. Is Erik here, too? Maybe I haven't spotted him yet. Otherwise, he's sitting in the quarry, waiting for me to speak. That's kind of comical.

Erma shakes her head. *I can't. But I was given permission to give you a glimpse.*

A glimpse? What if I want more than that? I reply. I may be whining.

You have no choice. Everything must obey the schedule.

What kind of schedule?

Instead of replying, Erma turns around. Is she looking for someone?

Is everyone on the same schedule? What about Erik? Is he here somewhere? Are we on the same schedule?

He gets no further than the stone, Erma replies.

Why? I ask, her words troubling to me.

YOU, MY CHILD, ASK A LOT OF QUESTIONS.

Chapter 8 - Why Not Erik?

I turn at the voice. A golden blob I hadn't seen before is whirling, whirling, whirling, into Grandfatherly Figure! He's starting to walk with me. Erma's slowed down into a skip behind us. And behind her are the gray blobs.

YOU WANT TO KNOW TOO MUCH TOO SOON, Grandfatherly Figure tells me, but he's looking straight ahead. When I follow his glance, all I see is sand or stardust except way, way off in the distance, where there's a rainbow, the sharpest, most beautiful rainbow I've ever seen.

THE STAGE IS STILL BEING SET FOR HUMAN BEINGS TO MOVE ON, Grandfatherly Figure continues. *THEY'RE ONE OF MANY SPECIES TO MATURE IN THIS UNIVERSE ON A SCHEDULE WE MUST KEEP. OTHERWISE, WHAT CHAOS!*

He laughs and his whole face lights up. I'd like to make him laugh again. But he's saying stuff similar to what the Overlords say in *Childhood's End*. Is this my imagination? Or perhaps the book is real?

Is maturing like evolving? Lots of questions come to me, but that's the one I ask.

SMART GIRL. YES, HUMANS ARE EVOLVING VERY NICELY. SOON THEY'LL BE AWAKE AND READY TO LEARN HOW TO STEWARD THEIR PLANET AND THEIR STAR SYSTEM.

They're asleep? I'm just trying to get things straight.

THEY'RE LIVING A STORY. HISTORY HAS BEEN THEIR TEETHING RING, Grandfatherly Figure says, then laughs. *IF THEY DON'T WAKE UP SOON, THEY MIGHT DESTROY EARTH TOTALLY! I'D GET IN A LOT OF TROUBLE IF THAT HAPPENED.*

Quarry Face

I'm listening to every word he's saying and carefully, too, but I'm still confused.

As if he's read my mind, which I guess makes sense since he's in it, he says, *YOU WILL HEAR MY WORDS; THEY MAY NOT MEAN VERY MUCH TO YOU TODAY, BUT THEY WILL COME BACK TO YOU MANY ORBITS FROM NOW WHEN YOU ARE READY TO ACT ON THEM.*

Are you an alien? I ask. Is that what I'm talking to? Aliens in my head?

I AM ENERGY, LIKE YOU, Grandfatherly Figure replies.

Okay, somehow that makes sense to me.

I AM GIVING YOU A GLIMPSE OF THE FUTURE SO YOU STAY HOPEFUL AS HISTORY WINDS UP. IT MAY BE ROUGH, MY CHILD, BUT THE TRANSITION AFTERWARDS WILL BE VERY SWIFT. YOU WILL BE HAPPY WITH THE WORLD IT BRINGS YOU AND YOUR DESCENDANTS.

He makes a sweeping motion with his hand so that I look around, 360 degrees, from the bright rainbow ahead of us, to the sand or stardust on both sides to Erma and the blobs behind me, and everywhere I turn I feel love, pure love. It's like what I feel when Mom hugs me, only a million times stronger, as if every generation of women in my family past, present, and future are giving me one gigantic group embrace.

Grandfatherly Figure continues. *YOU ARE WITNESSING YOUR SUBCONSCIOUS JOURNEY HOME. OTHERS ARE ALSO EN ROUTE, BUT THEY ARE NOT AWARE OF WHAT IS HAPPENING. AND THAT, MY CHILD, IS ALL FOR NOW. TOO MUCH TOO SOON COULD DAMAGE YOUR*

Chapter 8 - Why Not Erik?

NERVOUS SYSTEM. BESIDES, HUMANS NEED A NEW VOCABULARY TO COMMUNICATE PROPERLY WITH US.

We're still walking, Grandfatherly Figure and me. There's so much I want to ask, even if he thinks he's said enough. But before I do that, I've got a question that won't go away.

What about Erik? Why isn't he here with me? Why can't he go further than the stone?

Grandfatherly Figure stops. I stop, too. So do Erma and the blobs. Hey, that sounds like a rock and roll band!

THE SACRED SEED IS WITHIN YOU, THE SEED AND THE STORY, Grandfatherly Figure says.

My goose bumps just got goose bumps. But still— *How do I know I'm not imagining you, like those kids in Medjugorje imagine seeing the Virgin Mary?*

THERE ARE MANY PATHS TO WHERE YOU MUST GO, Grandfatherly Figure replies, and with that, he touches my shoulder.

I jump. At least, I feel like I do, even if only in my mind. He removes his hand. I still feel a shock. Before I can tell him that, Grandfatherly Figure turns and nods at Erma. She gives us both a gigantic smile, then snaps her fingers.

My eyes open wide. Erik's staring at me. We're in the quarry.

"You spacing out, Princess?"

Quarry Face

Erik looks as real as before. The boulder looks real. The flower. Once again, was I dreaming? Or is this the dream? How long have I been gone?

"Yo, King!"

"Yo, Jimbo," Erik yells out, waving at his friend.

"Hi, Jimmy!" I wave, too, as Jimmy rides his bike past that sliver of road above. And when he's out of sight, I turn to Erik to ask how long my eyes were shut. His expression scares me.

"What's wrong?"

"It's probably just my imagination," he replies, but with a worried look.

"What is?"

He shrugs and shakes his head, like he doesn't want to tell me. A second later, he says, "Something's bugging me about Jimbo, all these weird questions he's started asking."

"You mean, like will God ever come back to Earth?"

"Yeah, exactly. Well, no, but, well yeah. It's not like we don't have sermons in church about Jesus returning someday. I guess what's bothering me is how obsessed he is with his questions lately. He's been weird ever since we stopped and talked to those Joy Star crazies," he says and shakes his head again.

"I remember seeing them when you and I were in Carmel Plaza. Martha said Jimmy asked her the same kind of stuff."

Chapter 8 - Why Not Erik?

"Yeah, he hasn't been the same since the day we goofed around with them. I was just joking, asking them what they believe in," Erik continues. "But Jimbo got into a big discussion about why they think Joy Star is God, and he's been acting strange ever since. It's like he believed them."

"At least he hasn't joined them."

"He'd better not!" Erik balls up his hands.

I can't help flinching.

Erik unfurls his fists and laughs. "Hey, don't worry. I wouldn't hurt Jimbo. He's like a brother. But it's wise not to mess with me, Princess."

"Princess," I repeat, not sure how to take that.

"Yeah, Jolie Princess Rich. Now you've got a middle name, like you always wanted," he says.

"Just for that, I'll let you in on a secret." I lower my voice. "This flower is magical. If you kiss it, whatever you wish comes true."

"You mean it?" Erik asks, grinning. "That could get you in a lot of trouble."

"That's okay." I keep a straight face, so he doesn't think I got his sexual connotation. He sounded cute, even if I don't think guys should make sexual remarks and despite Martha's warning.

In case even an iota of what I told him is true, I bend over and gently kiss the flower, while I silently pray, *I wish for peace on Earth and everywhere else in the universe.*

Quarry Face

"Perfect! Don't make a move."

"You're such a sneak, Marco!" I say, as I quickly sit back up.

Neither of us saw him coming. He's much braver with his camera today. He's in the water, while holding it steady on Harry's float.

"Can you two get a little closer?" he asks, and motions how he means.

Erik's arm feels nice around my shoulder. I may be blushing. He's got long, thin fingers. They're a little yellow, though. Nobody should smoke.

"I don't mean to be a nuisance," Marco says, as he snaps more photos, "but I've got a great idea for a photography book of the quarry. The magazine article got me started, but with Jolie, the project's taking on a life of its own."

Does that mean my photo will be in a book? Erik's too? Do we look like a couple of typical teenagers to Marco? I don't feel like a typical anything right now. Was I somewhere else than on Earth just minutes ago?

"I'd never take chances like that with an expensive camera," Erik tells me, after Marco starts paddling off with Harry. My brother's waving like they're going on a long journey.

"Me neither," I agree, but my mind's somewhere else. Did Grandfatherly Figure say that Erik's not ready? And what about me? How come I got kicked out again?

Chapter 8 - Why Not Erik?

"Princess, you think too much," Erik says, leaning in, his lips suddenly tickling my left ear.

"Don't," I say moving away. Just then, a question I'd wanted to ask before pops into my head. "Erik, remember the other night, when you said your dad's death was like getting excused from this rathole? What did you mean?"

"Jesus, girl, you sure know how to ruin a mood!" Erik says.

Marco's whistling. We both look over. He's waving for us to follow.

"Must be time for the frogs," I say, sorry for yet another interruption.

Erik stands up. I do too. So, was I told something about sacred seeds and stories? Or did I imagine it all? Erik quickly unties his raft. Then he jumps over to it and reaches back for my hand. As I take it, the bellowing starts.

Chapter 9
Jimbo's Jolt

> *Soft, but commanding,*
> *The signal draws near,*
> *Its tone energizing,*
> *Its hope crystal clear.*
>   Jolie Rich
>   Carmel, New York

As much as I hate going to The Video Palace, here I am with Harry. He's my excuse. He's heading right where I knew he would, paying no mind to the other games, the flashing lights, or the incredibly loud buzzing, beeping, and music.

Erik looks down as soon as Harry taps his arm.

"Hey, it's the Quarry Kid," he says, then glances over at me.

"Hi," I say with a wave, but he's already turned back to the screen.

"Oh, shit," he says a second later.

His frog must have gotten zapped in traffic.

Chapter 9 - Jimbo's Jolt

"Shit's right," Dominick's saying when I reach everyone. The girls I met before are here, too, but not Bobby.

"Shit!" Harry repeats.

I put my hand over his mouth. He quickly pulls it off.

"You should never turn away from the screen, Princess," Erik says, his glance going from me to his friends. "Never. Let my mistake be a lesson to all of you."

They all laugh, of course. But his look at me confirms what I thought. Just because I wanted him to call was no reason he would. He probably didn't have any better time with me than I had with him in the quarry. Yet I needed to see him again. Don't ask me why, I just did. I couldn't get him out of my mind. Well, now I'll have to try harder. I'll give Harry money for one game, so it isn't obvious why we're here. Then we'll go.

"Hey, you hear about Jimmy?"

Bobby's running towards us, panting out his news.

"Hear what about Jimbo?" Erik asks.

Between huffs, Bobby says, "He ran off…to join…Joy Star."

"Don't mess with me, man. I saw him yesterday. He sounded a little weird, but then he always does," Erik says with a laugh that sounds forced to me.

"Yeah, well, go ask my mom," says Bobby. "She took my Aunt Valerie to see his shop. They think it's so cute that he serves free lemonade. Knowing my aunt, she probably figured he didn't know his ass from his antiques—pardon my French, ladies— so she'd get some great bargains. But Jimmy's mom said he'd split."

"And get this," Bobby continues. "He left a note saying she should keep the profits from Poorboy, because he'd found the *real* prophet. Get it? P-r-o-however you spell the prophet that predicts the future. My mom said it was bad enough when he ran off to join the Marines. At least then his parents knew he'd be back, because he was too young to enlist. But Joy Star takes anyone. They sign over trust funds to him and everything."

Andi giggles, "If they think Jimmy's rich, they're in for a big surprise."

"Why didn't he speak to me first?" Erik shakes his head.

Poor Erik. His dad died. Now his best friend's run off without telling him.

"You know where to find them?" Andi asks, punching the air like a boxer. "If you do, we can rescue him."

"Solomon Hill," Bobby says.

"What! You're screwing with me, aren't you?" Erik says.

"Don't any of you meatheads read *The Carmel Patent Trader*?" Bobby asks. "Okay, neither do I, but my mom said she read an article in it yesterday about Joy Star buying that old mansion on Solomon Hill and moving his group into it."

"The bastard," Erik mutters.

Chapter 9 - Jimbo's Jolt

"Jimmy's probably there right now wondering what he got himself into," Andi says. "We've got to rescue him right away."

She's added fancy footwork to her air punches. She's so cute. Maybe Erik likes her. I wouldn't blame him, not that looks should matter, of course.

Dominick shakes his head. "They've probably got guard dogs all around the place. Sorry, but I'm not getting mauled over Jimmy. He could have walked away from them like I did. Like you did, King."

Grandfatherly Figure pops into my head, as he has many times this week. Pops in, then pops out. His words are like a gold ring on a carousel, within reach yet beyond my grasp. I need Marco to get back to Carmel so he can take us to the quarry again, but he's on a photo shoot, this one in Costa Rica. He said they don't have an army there, and everyone's into ecology. I'd love to go there someday. Paris, too. Actually, I'd love to go everywhere and write about everywhere I go. I've written about where I went when I sat on Sunwake, but I turned it into a short story, so nobody would think I'd lost my mind.

"But you know Jimbo. He's always looking for something to believe in," Erik's saying when I force my mind to stop wandering.

"I gotta split!" Andi says and starts walking backwards towards the door. "But if any of you get a brainstorm, count me in. I'm serious. Oh, excuse me."

The manager shakes his head after Andi bumps into him. Then he looks towards the rest of us and yells, "How many times must I tell you, no smoking in here? I lose my license if they catch you."

"Sure, sure, boss," Erik says, crushing his cigarette beneath his sneaker. "C'mon, let's split. Anyway, I've got to get to work."

The rest of us follow, except Carrie, who's staying to wait for a friend.

Once outside, Bobby runs off to meet his dad at the barber. Harry wants to run ahead, which I say he can if he stays in sight. I watch him as I walk along with Dominick and Erik. For a while none of us speak. Then Erik snaps his fingers.

"I've got it."

"Is it contagious?" Dominick asks.

Erik lowers his voice, "We should burn down Joy Star's headquarters. That's what we should do."

"C'mon," Dominick replies. "That's a joke, right, King?"

"I'm serious. We should burn the place to the ground," Erik says, then stops talking while a woman pushing a baby stroller approaches. She smiles. We all smile back. When she's out of hearing range, Erik continues. "If all we do is rescue Jimbo, Joy Star will still be in Carmel, brainwashing others into joining his cult, calling him God, and giving him everything they own. He's evil, man. He should know he's not welcome in Carmel."

"But you'll go to jail and people could get hurt," I say.

Chapter 9 - Jimbo's Jolt

Maybe Erik's just trying to be funny or act like a big shot, but if he's serious, he shouldn't be! And even if nobody gets hurt, you don't burn down people's property because you disagree with them. Besides, that's the house Erik's dad wanted. Doesn't that matter to him? Or maybe that's why he's so upset.

"I'll be careful, Mommy, honest I will," Erik laughs.

Dominick does, too.

I can't tell if Erik's serious. He's making faces—nodding and shaking his head and smiling and frowning—like he's having a meeting inside his mind, like he's got a whole committee up there. Dominick's still laughing. I'm trying not to.

When we reach Putnam Pets, I motion for Harry to catch up to us. I know what he'd prefer, but I shake my head. He knows to obey. He gets 10 cents a day if I say he's been good. It works.

At the corner, the light's turning red. Erik looks like he's about to run across the street.

"Hey, Erik? Come over to my house tomorrow," I quickly say. I can't let him just leave.

"Me?" He motions to himself with what looks like a smirk. "You want me to come to your house tomorrow? Did I hear right?"

I nod. I've got to watch Harry, so the easiest place to talk is the cottage, not that I'm sure what I'll say, just that I've got to say something. It's silly, I guess, and I can't explain why, but he matters to me. I don't want him doing anything stupid or dangerous.

Erik breaks into a run. He's in the middle of the road when he looks back at me and shouts, "What time, Princess?"

"Two o'clock," I yell back. I think that's about a half hour before Erik goes to work.

"Make it two-thirty," he replies, then starts running faster.

Just as he gets to the other side, the light turns green for traffic.

"You think he's serious?" I ask Dominick, while we wait to go. My stomach's feeling queasy, like it did this morning when I decided to try to see Erik, or how it gets every night when my dad calls and Mom whispers to me, "At least say *hello* to him."

"The King's unpredictable. You never know what he'll do next."

"Why's he nicknamed The King?" I ask.

"You'll have to ask him," Dominick says, as the light turns red and we start running across.

I wait until we're on the other side, Harry having reluctantly held my hand, before I ask Dominick, "So how do you reason with him?"

"You don't. It's a waste of time. He's the type of guy who has to learn from his own mistakes."

Chapter 9 - Jimbo's Jolt

I don't get it. How can Dominick be so calm when his friend's plotting a crime? Even if Erik doesn't mean to hurt anyone, things can go wrong. I've seen TV shows where that happens. Someone just wants to scare someone else, but the plan backfires, and they wind up killing people or getting killed.

If I care about Erik, I've got to try to reason with him.

Chapter 10
The Jerk

> I've reached a strange familiar place
> In The Quarry and also in space,
> On a wavelength I can find
> Beyond the borders of my mind.
>   Jolie Rich
>   Carmel, New York

"Hey— Oh, I'm sorry. I didn't mean to scare you," Marco says, my front door slamming behind him.

"I thought you weren't coming back until tomorrow," I say, clutching my heart. I must have jumped a few inches from the couch when he ran in just now.

"My shoot ended early. So, anyone here want to go to the quarry in ten minutes?"

"Me, me, me!" Harry yells, running in from the kitchen.

What a mess! He's got finger paint all over him, but that's okay. It'll all wash off and I got a chance to write. But nothing's ready to be seen. I cover my journal with my hands.

"Please, Jojo, say we can go. Please."

Chapter 10 - The Jerk

"You can go. Just make sure you wear your water wings, and wash your—"

Before I can finish, Harry's grabbed his swim trunks from Mom's bedroom and run into the bathroom.

Marco's been gone a whole week and a half this time. Darn! I sit up straighter, sure this will hurt me more than him. "I'd love to go with you, but I can't today."

Marco looks surprised. "You sure? How come?"

"It's personal...Harry, you stop that!"

Harry's giggling in the bathroom.

Marco looks at me quizzically, but I'm not about to explain what's going on. Lucky for me, the next instant Harry's out of the bathroom, soap still on his arms, and I've got to help him finish cleaning up. Then, without waiting for Marco, he dashes outside, water wings in hand. Marco starts after him, then stops and turns to me.

"I nearly forgot. Mira phoned yesterday and asked if you started reading *Childhood's End*."

"Tell her I finished it last night!" I say. I didn't think I would, but then I got to this part where a kid hears an Overlord's voice in his head and it reminded me of the quarry, of course, and I couldn't put it down. I stayed up real late to see how it ended. "I was so excited about the Overlords coming and bringing a Golden Age to Earth, but the end was so sad—"

Just thinking about it gives me the chills.

Quarry Face

"I read it a long time ago, but you can tell me what you thought when we go to Bannerman's Arsenal tomorrow," Marco replies.

"Where?"

"Bannerman's Arsenal. It's an island in the Hudson River."

"The Hudson River has islands?" This I did not know.

Marco nods. "And this one's particularly interesting. I told a writer friend I'd take some shots of kids there for an article he's doing. I'll check with your mom later to make sure it's okay with her. You get to cross the Hudson in my boat."

"You've got a boat?" More news I did not know.

"To be honest, it's more like a rubber canoe, but it'll be fun. You'll see."

"I'd much rather go to the quarry. I'd go today, except—" I shrug, since I can't say I'm waiting for a guy or why.

Hey, I made a rhyme! Erma would be proud of me.

"Well, I can really use those shots. Listen, if there's time afterwards tomorrow, I promise we'll go to the quarry. Anyway, you'll like Bannerman's Arsenal. It'll give you some great ideas for poems."

"C'mon, Marco! Let's go!" Harry yells outside.

"I'm being paged," Marco says with a laugh, as the door slams behind him.

Chapter 10 - The Jerk

Soon I can hear Marco's wheels crunching gravel.

This is a bit weird. I thought Harry would be with me when Erik came. But I'm alone now and it's two-fifteen. No sense trying to write any more. And I'm too anxious to try any ESP. I'm up to Test #106. Still no success. Still feel I've got to try. So, what was Aunt Tish's tip for relieving stress? She said to take five deep breaths.

Here goes: one, two, threee, foooour, fiiiiiiiiiiiiive.

Well, that didn't work.

Cleaning up Harry's mess in the bathroom takes a long five minutes. Maybe there's something to read, but nothing deep. And no more science fiction. I don't want to mix up *Childhood's End* with anything else. I need to think about it more.

There's not much in my aunt's bookcase. She and Chuck probably keep their best books at their apartment in Manhattan. Oh, here's something. The cover shows a sexy teenage couple kissing as they lean over a cake with sixteen candles. Not exactly a *Childhood's End*. It's called *Sweet Sixteen* and the author is Natalie Taxel. That's the name Aunt Tish used when she wrote romances to make money before she could afford to just shoot documentaries. I told her I hoped I didn't have to write stuff I wouldn't publish under my own name. She said she hoped my wish came true.

It's two-thirty. Might as well wait outside.

As soon as I open the door, guess what?

Quarry Face

"Hi," I call out, because Erik's wheeling his bike through the bushes.

~

He's right on time. I wasn't sure he'd come at all, which I guess is why the next thing I say is, "You came!"

"I said I would," he replies when he reaches the stoop. Then he sort of chuckles and points at my aunt's garden. "My dad always loved telling the story of how Mom planted too much squash the first year they got married. They wound up with enough to feed an army. Every spring after that, he'd kid her about her first garden. And she always laughed, like she was hearing his story for the first time."

He lays his bike on the grass, then straightens up and asks, "So, where is everyone, Princess?"

"My mom's working, and Marco just left for the quarry with Harry."

He's got this sly smile as he sits down on the stoop. Wait a minute! Does he think I planned this so we could be alone?

He takes out his cigarette pack and holds it out to me.

"I still don't smoke," I say. And I'm about to tell him not to get the wrong idea about why I've asked him over when he grabs *Sweet Sixteen* from my hand.

"So this is what you read when I'm not around?" he says, like we're an old married couple.

I can't help but smile. I'm glad he came. Looks should not matter, but his light blue t-shirt makes his eyes look extra

Chapter 10 - The Jerk

blue today. My grandma, the one who loves us, (not my dad's mom who hates all kids), told me she wanted to marry someone with blue eyes, because hers are brown. She also wanted someone with a better nose than hers. Then she met my grandpa and decided to go with just a good nose. "That's why you, Harry, and your mom don't have big schnozzles like mine," she's told me more than once. "And that's how come I had forty wonderful years with Sol, God rest his soul." She always says I'd have loved my grandpa. He was a very quiet man, but a good one.

"The most sensual story ever written about first love," Erik reads from the cover. Then he opens to the first page. "'There'll never be a second time like the first,' she said." He's using a high-pitched voice, like a woman's.

"It's not exactly a classic. And I wasn't really reading—"

"That's what they all say," Erik replies, handing me back the book. He lights his cigarette while I shrug, unsure how to respond. "But what I want to know is whether it's true. Ever been in love, Princess?"

Right away I think of a certain boy in homeroom last fall. He dressed like a stuffed laundry bag, his shirt always falling out of his pants, and his pants loose like a clown's. He wasn't good-looking, but that didn't matter, and it wasn't that I even wanted to go out with him. But I felt happy whenever I saw him, and everything he said sounded funny to me. I asked Aunt Tish how you know a crush from love. She said when you find your soul mate, you know it, and realize that what you felt for guys before were just crushes. After spring break, when I saw my "crush" in school again, I didn't feel any attraction anymore. What had seemed funny now seemed stupid.

Quarry Face

"Have you?" Erik asks again.

"I guess not. Why? Have you ever been in love?"

"I don't believe in love."

"That's ridiculous. Does that mean you don't believe in hate, either?"

Erik chuckles. He blows a smoke ring in the air. We both watch in silence as it gets bigger and bigger, then starts fading away. I wonder why that happens. I guess a scientist would know.

"Okay, let me give you an example of why I think love's not real," he replies when the ring's nearly gone. "I've got an older brother, right? Jeff's a chemist and a great guy. His girlfriend, Lala, is always saying how much she loves him. But then, while he's in China at a science convention, Lala and Jeff's best friend—his best friend, mind you—sleep together. And when he finds out about it, they both swear it meant absolutely nothing, it just happened. Dinner together, a few drinks, then…wham!"

He claps. I jump. That's twice today.

Erik continues, "I asked Jeff, 'What are they, animals? How can she claim to love you and have sex with your buddy behind your back?' Man, I can tell my brother's hurt, although he tries not to show it. But if that's love, screw it. And then there's my mom. My dad's buried less than a year and already she's dating some baker in Brewster! Big Al, that's his nickname. Big Al!"

He extends his hands to give me an idea of size.

Chapter 10 - The Jerk

"Maybe she's lonely. Is Big Al a good baker?" I ask. "That could be a bonus."

"A bonus," Erik repeats, looking like he's trying not to smile. "Hey, you got anything to drink?"

Without waiting for my answer, he gets up and opens my front door. Shouldn't he ask first? I follow him inside.

"Mind if I open the fridge?" he asks in the kitchen.

Could I say no? "Help yourself."

He chooses a can of Coke, pops it open, takes a long swallow, and makes a fake belch. What is it with guys? Then he leans against the stove, and pushing his hair from over his eyes, asks, "So, why did you ask me over?"

Showtime.

"I wanted to talk to you about the guru." Yuck! My voice sounds super whiny.

"The guru is thu-ru," Erik says, pulling something from his back pocket. "Here, Princess. You might enjoy this."

It's a newspaper article. I read the headline aloud. "Joy Star Junkies Jailed."

Erik's heading for the living room. I follow, clipping in hand.

He sits down on the couch and says, "It's about Joy Star followers upstate in Kingston who got arrested for disturbing the peace with their chanting. My mom gave it to me. She heard about Jimmy from his mom, and now she'll clip out every article she sees about Joy Star. That and my daily horoscope."

"Your horoscope? Really?" How can anyone believe in newspaper horoscopes?

Erik laughs. "My mom believes in astrology and past life regression and fortune tellers and psychic phenomena, all that crap. She takes fortune cookies very seriously, too," he sighs, as though his mom's a child to him.

I've got to stay focused. No going off on tangents. Although it's just us two, I keep my voice low. "So, were you serious about what you said you're going to do?"

"You mean my little plan?" Erik leans forward. "Actually, it doesn't have to be so little. We can start with Joy Star in Carmel, and if we're successful, we can roll it out across the country, wherever creeps who claim to be God prey on people. Did I say 'country?' Well, excuse me! We can rid the whole world of phony prophets. All we'll need are some good alibis and a lot of matches."

He can't be serious, can he? I feel like laughing, but I've got to be the voice of reason. Otherwise, I might as well be climbing down the hill to the quarry right now.

"What if something goes wrong and innocent people get hurt?"

"Princess, don't you think I'll be careful? I'm just so pissed at Jimbo," Erik replies, making two fists and scrunching his face like a mean boxer. Then he releases his fists, and pats the couch. "Come, sit down here and we'll talk."

Chapter 10 - The Jerk

I didn't plan this out very well. Maybe because I doubted he'd really show.

Erik pats the couch again, "C'mon, sit down and we'll talk, scout's honor. Hey, did I ever tell you how I got kicked out of Cub Scouts?"

"You turn everything into a joke," I say, as I sit down a good distance from him.

"And you take everything way too seriously. You keep that up, you'll have a heart attack before you turn— Hey, that's the shirt I like. The one that reminds me of Eve," Erik says, while propping two pillows behind his head.

Then he gulps down more soda at once than I've ever seen anyone do before. He finishes, pounds his chest, and belches once more.

"Ah, that felt good," he says, and the way his eyes twinkle and he laughs makes his being uncouth cute. That's ridiculous! Besides, I've got no time to joke around.

"Erik, I wish you'd be serious. If you commit arson, you'll be making a big mistake."

"I'm only human, Princess. Humans make big mistakes. Hey, ever see this trick?"

With that, he crushes his empty soda can against his forehead.

Jump three for me. Erik's laughing, while I'm clutching my chest.

'No, I guess you haven't," he says, and then, without warning, he's leaning way over and pressing his lips against mine, while pinning down my shoulders with his hands.

"No, Erik—" I push him away.

"So, when are they, you know, getting back?" he asks, standing up.

"Very soon." He's scaring me. Pants. Bulge. Weird sensation. Danger.

"Then maybe we should go, you know." He's motioning towards Mom's bedroom. The door's open. I see her bed from here.

"Why?" I ask, surprised that a part of me wants him to take me there.

"I can show you a few pointers on how to lighten up," Erik says, reaching for my hand.

My body's tingling as I pull both hands behind my back.

"But we like each other," he says.

"C'mon, please don't," I say and move farther away on the couch.

Martha says guys will lie to get what they want and most want just one thing. That's what's running through my mind when Erik speaks again.

"Anyway, Princess, the Dark Ages are over."

"Why? Did someone turn on the light?" I ask.

Chapter 10 - The Jerk

Erik drops his cigarette into his crushed soda can and stands up.

"Did someone turn on the light?" he repeats. "That's a good one. Well, suit yourself, Princess. It's your loss."

"Wait, don't go. I wanted us to talk."

"You're all the same. You invite a guy over, tease the hell out of him, and then say, 'Oh, no, I'm not like that.' Thanks, Princess. Good show."

"I didn't ask you over to tease you," I say as he taps out a cigarette from his pack.

"Then what did you call that kiss? You know you kissed me back."

"I did not." Did I? I might have. His lips. Goose bumps.

Erik lights up, then pulls out a watch face from his back pocket. "Wouldn't have had time anyway. Gotta split. Promised manager, who happens to have seven kids, I'd come in a little early. But, just for the record, asking me over was asking for trouble."

He's heading for the door now.

"But I felt like someone should try to tell you—"

Suddenly I freeze. Erik's just like my dad. Neither of them wants to hear me.

"There's nothing to talk about, Princess. It's a done deal," Erik says at the door.

Quarry Face

The sun makes me squint as I follow him outside.

"Well, see you around," he says, picking up his bike from the grass. "I'll tell Joy Star you put in a good word for him."

The best I can do, and it's not until he's about to wheel his bike through the bushes, is yell out, "You're not funny!"

He doesn't look back. No one-finger wave. Soon he's out of sight. I rush inside to the kitchen window. He's pedaling towards McDonald's. He's getting blurry, the big idiot. Oh, I hope he doesn't do something stupid.

Hope? What a lame word. Hope doesn't make people change, does it? So, what does? Prayer? I suppose that's what everyone thinks in Medjugorje. The Overlords? Sure, they changed people's minds, but they're only characters in a novel. Besides, they came to Earth to supervise its end, which I don't want to think about. Nor do I want to think about Erik, but I am. It's not just because I worry about him committing a crime. As much as I hate to admit it, when he kissed me, it felt good. And just seeing him gets me all tingly inside.

But that's ridiculous. I'm not interested in boys yet, am I? But—just say I am—why would I like someone who's only interested in sex, not in me?

Why do I hear Aunt Tish in my head, saying "You just know."

Shouldn't love be a smart choice? I wonder what Grandfatherly Figure and Erma would say about it.

Chapter 11
War & Peace

> The smarter you are,
> The sooner you'll know
> When it's time to wake up
> So Earth's future can grow.
> Jolie Rich
> Carmel, New York

"There, Marco, over there!" I shout, having spotted the kind of landing I think he meant I should find. He and Harry did the rowing. And I'm amazed, because there really are islands in the Hudson. And this one's got a castle!

After maneuvering his yellow rubber canoe to where I'm pointing, Marco gives me a puzzled look. Then he starts climbing out.

A second later, he says, "Oh, no!"

"Oh, I'm so sorry," I say, but I can't help laughing. Neither can Harry.

"The ground looked firm to me."

Quarry Face

"Well, guess what?" Marco says, his left foot in mud up to his calf.

He sticks his other foot in the mud and pulls the canoe onto more solid ground before letting us get out. Then we all drag the canoe up further so Marco can tie it to a tree. He insists we clean the muck from our shoes before going on.

"I made a lousy Girl Scout," I mutter, but I'm serious. I joined the Girl Scouts more for Mom than for me. I lasted two years. Oh, I hope we get back to the quarry today. I know I was told not to return to Sunwake, but I still want to try. I miss the feeling I got with Grandfatherly Figure and Erma.

I stand up as soon as Marco says he's ready to move on. Harry does, too.

Marco takes the lead, heading toward the castle. It looks dilapidated now, like it's all in ruins.

"Check this out, guys," he calls out as we're getting closer.

From here, the castle looks like it's made of lots of boulders all cemented together.

Marco's stopped in front of a doorframe, a very old one. No door. Just an opening outlined in splintered, weathered wood. I'm the last to go through it. So now we're standing at one end of a huge open space with no roof overhead, and bunches of rusty objects on the ground. What looked like a castle when we crossed the Hudson now looks more like a stage set.

Chapter 11 - War & Peace

Harry scoops up something from the dirt, hands it to Marco and asks, "Hey, what is this?"

"Looks like a belt buckle. There are millions of them here. They were used on ammunition belts," Marco replies.

"What happened to this place, anyway?" I ask. Ammunition belts?

"Gigantic fire," Marco says, raising his camera to his eye.

"Fire!" I practically screech.

"Fire! Fire!" Harry yells.

"Uh huh. Must have been an amazing blaze. I think it happened sometime in the late 1960s. I don't know all the details."

Well, that's a relief. Erik hadn't been born yet. I turn away so Marco won't keep shooting me.

"Hey, let's try that opening," I say, pointing towards a rocky section that looks like it might lead to a balcony.

Marco nods, and leads again. Harry's behind him, and I'm in the rear as we climb up a broken stairway until we reach what does seem like the remains of a balcony overlooking the Hudson. Maybe people ate lunch here while watching boats go by. It must have been very peaceful.

For a while, we're all silent, even Harry. He's facing the sky with his eyes shut and a big smile. Marco shoots his picture. Right now, my brother looks like a poster child for "it's good to be alive!" If I listen, I can hear some birds fluttering around and buoys gently bobbing in the water.

Brrrrrr-brrrrrr-brrrrrr. Power boat going by. Brrrrrr-brrrrrr-brrrrrr. Another one.

"Let's go there, Marco," I say, heading back inside. "Let me lead this time."

Marco extends his arm like "be my guest," so I start walking up some uneven steps with him and Harry following. Marco's clicking away.

"Hey, what's this?" Harry says.

Marco and I stop and turn.

"Probably the frame from an ammunition box," Marco says, seeing where Harry's pointing.

"An ammunition box?" An instant later I feel like smacking my forehead. "Now I get it. They made ammunition here. You kept saying Bannerman's Arsenal, but the word 'arsenal' didn't hit me until right now. What an idiot."

"Actually, they just *stored* ammo here. The name came from Francis Bannerman, who built the arsenal in the early 1900s," Marco says, as he sits down on a pile of jagged red bricks.

This looks like the highest we can go. I sit down too, and take a few sips from the water canteen I'm wearing around my waist. Harry takes a swig as well and then heads back to where he'd been scavenging.

Chapter 11 - War & Peace

"I hate anything having to do with ammunition, with people killing each other," I tell Marco, now that he's lowered his camera, although it's probably just for a second. "I loved when the Overlords came to Earth in *Childhood's End* because they put an end to all kinds of violence— Marco, stop it! I can't think straight when I have to talk to a camera the entire time."

"I'm sorry." Marco lowers his Nikon again. "Please, go on."

I look over at Harry. He's still rummaging through the rubble, a big smile on his face.

"I loved the story, but it was dated," I tell Marco. "I'm sure that technology's much more advanced than when it was written 30 years ago. And a lot of it takes place in the 21st century, but he's still got people smoking cigarettes."

"Old habits die hard."

"I can't believe people won't be more concerned about their health by the 21st century. Oh, but didn't the ending make you want to cry?"

"Like I said, I read it a long time ago."

"I'll *never* forget it. Never, as long as I live. At the end, the generation the Overlords were waiting for is born, and its children form one powerful mind, an energy source that destroys Earth as the planet was always destined to be destroyed one day. Now is it coming back to you?"

Marco clears his throat. "Don't forget, it's science fiction, not fact."

Quarry Face

"But it's possible, isn't it? I mean, visitors from another planet could come here and change how people act, couldn't they?"

Marco sighs, "The older I get, the more skeptical I am that people can change, whether because of aliens from space or leaders on Earth." He points his camera at Harry. "Anyway, I don't expect extraterrestrials here any time soon. It's not exactly a hop, skip, and a jump to travel between stars. They're trillions of miles apart. Furthermore, nobody knows for sure yet if other planets even *exist* beyond the Solar System.

"The Solar System can't be the *only* place where there are planets in the universe. It doesn't make any sense."

Marco laughs as he stands up.

"I'm a scientist, Jolie. I don't believe anything unless I see the proof, the hard evidence," he says, tapping his fingers of one hand into the palm of the other.

No sense saying a peep to him about Sunwake.

He motions for us to follow him down, back towards the ground level. This time Harry skips on ahead now that we know the way. I'm glad he's having fun.

"Hey, look what I found!" he giggles, stopping to raise something in the air.

It's green, but I can't tell what it is from here.

"It's a plastic toy army tank," Marco says when we get closer. "Some kid must have dropped it on a visit here. Take it home as a souvenir, mate. And so much for your

Chapter 11 - War & Peace

Overlords, Jolie. Cavemen had their clubs. We've got our tanks and nuclear bombs and in the next few years, we'll have weapons in space. War is in our genes. We'll be lucky if some nut doesn't blow up the whole planet long before we ever get the chance to contact intelligent beings from space." Marco finishes with a slight laugh. But then he adds, "Although, if they're intelligent, they'll probably want nothing to do with us."

Harry's walked on ahead. Even so, I lower my voice to say, "I don't get it, Marco. Why would God create a beautiful planet like Earth, and then let people destroy it?"

"Who says there's a God?" Marco replies. Then he stops walking and shakes his head. "Hey, I'm sorry. I shouldn't have said that."

"No, that's okay. I don't know that I believe in God either, not with so much wrong with this world. A real God would fix things, wouldn't he?" I ask.

"You would think," Marco replies.

Neither of us know much, do we? That's what I'm thinking when Grandfatherly Figure and Erma pop into my head. The Overlords too. They seemed so real while I was reading *Childhood's End*. And I cared what happened to them, not just to humans on Earth. They seemed genuinely sad to be the ones to tell humans that their children were no longer their own. I know, I know. It just a story, but it felt so real.

Marco clears his throat. "If it's any consolation, Jolie, you're not alone. Lots of smart people are confused about whether to believe in God or not. And then there are a lot of other people who very strongly believe in God, their particular God, but not anyone else's, and they'll fight wars over whose God is best.

"It's such a stupid...you know what," I reply. "I wish I could write like Arthur C. Clarke. I'd write a science fiction story in which all the countries on Earth become one, like in *Childhood's End,* only with a happy ending."

"You're a dreamer...like Mira," Marco says, smiling at me.

"That's right! She read *Childhood's End* and she likes my— Marco? Will she come up to Carmel before we go back to Brooklyn? I'd love to talk to her."

"I'm not sure. She's flying overseas tomorrow," he says.

"I'm sorry, Marco," I reply, because his face went all goofy just then.

"It's not your fault," he replies, raising his shoulders, then dropping them in the saddest shrug I've ever seen.

That does it! I can't let myself shrug like that about Erik. I've got to try to reason with him again. Grandfatherly Figure and Erma won't do it. And the Overlords aren't real. Besides, I feel like we're connected, Erik and me, like that couple Jeanne and her husband, George, in *Childhood's End.* Don't ask me why. I just do.

"That looks like a good spot to have lunch," Marco says, pointing to a shady tree near the bank of the Hudson. "And, Jolie, please forgive me, but right before we left I got a phone call about a pre-production meeting in Brewster tonight. We'll just have time to eat our sandwiches before heading back. I promise we'll go to the quarry tomorrow."

Chapter 11 - War & Peace

"Yay, let's eat!" yells Harry, clutching the toy tank and tugging at Marco's arm.

"Forgive me?" Marco asks, looking at me through his camera.

I nod, my hands over my face. No sad-faced pictures, please. And though I'm sure Marco means well, I won't be surprised if something comes up tomorrow that prevents him from keeping his promise. I'm learning that's the way of this stupid world. But that's okay because what I decided two minutes ago will get me to the quarry a lot sooner than Marco thinks.

Chapter 12
Quarry Starry Quarry

*Watch the past slip away
Like a thief in the dark,
As you climb aboard
Earth's mystery ark.*
    Jolie Rich
    Carmel, New York

"Call when you're ready for me to come get you. I'll be watching TV at your place until we hear from you."

"Thanks Marco," I say, as I slam his car door behind me.

Harry gives me a thumbs up from the back seat. Now two. Now a thumb dance.

"I'll phone by eleven, like I promised Mom," I say, then quickly thumb dance for Harry. He's giggling and tapping his wristwatch as Marco drives away.

I'm still in shock that Mom didn't argue when I asked to go to The Video Palace tonight. It's like I broke through an invisible barrier by having a date. She probably thinks I'm safe because I promised to stay at the Palace and let Marco

Chapter 12 - Quarry Starry Quarry

drive me there and back. I guess in this world sometimes you have to lie to do good things.

The flashing lights are blinding, and the noise level's deafening, as usual. But that's okay. I just have to find him. Yes, there he is. Froggers must be his favorite game. I'm glad I figured it right, that if Erik wasn't working tonight, he'd be here. Otherwise, I'd have gone to McDonald's after him. This time, just Dominick and Andi are watching him play. Dominick's got his arm around Andi. He's pulling her close and giving her a kiss. See, I knew it! I knew she had to be someone's girlfriend. She's so cute, and looks do matter.

I've been spotted. Dominick's tapping Erik's shoulder and pointing at me.

Erik quickly looks my way, then back at his game.

"Hey, it's the Princess," he says, his eyes on Froggers. Seconds later, the game ends. "All these machines are rigged. Or else I'm losing my touch."

I wiggle my backpack behind me to balance it better.

"You're a sore loser, King. You should be satisfied with second place," Andi says, motioning towards a list on Frogger's screen that I hadn't noticed before. It's got the names of the game's best players. Erik's in second place.

Dominick gives Andi's shoulder a squeeze.

"Erik, can we talk?" I ask, my voice not sounding at all like when I practiced.

"Talk? Talk?"

Quarry Face

His friends laugh.

"It's important," I say, refusing to smile at Erik's imitation of a squawking parrot. It's not easy keeping a straight face.

"Hey, lovebirds, it's all yours now. The Princess and I have got some business to attend to. We better step outside for this," Erik says.

Just as surprising, he holds the front door open for me.

"I don't do this for every chick."

"Don't worry, I know," I reply, and that's the last thing I say for a while.

I just walk along in silence while Erik pauses to light his cigarette and then continues on, me beside him. It was a lot easier knowing how to begin when I practiced in front of the bathroom mirror.

Erik puts his hand on my shoulder in front of Angela's Italian Deli. I lean my back against the store window, while he puts one foot on a water pipe sticking up from the ground.

"Okay, so what's up? You're not pregnant, are you? If you are, it wasn't me!"

I don't smile. "I'm not and I know that."

He's brushing his hair off his forehead again. He must like to do that or else maybe he knows it's cute. Otherwise, he could cut it short and be done with it. He's waiting for my response. Showtime again, but hopefully a better

Chapter 12 - Quarry Starry Quarry

production this time around. "The more I thought about your plan, the more I felt I had to try to stop you."

"Stop *me*? But you're okay with some con artist guru turning people's minds into mush and their money into mansions for him?" Erik stops and looks up at the sky. "Hey, that sounded pretty good, didn't it?"

I will not smile. I will not smile.

"But Joy Star's probably got some good points, too," I say, and cringe. Hearing my own words, I think I sounded very stupid just now.

"I bet that's what Hitler's friends said. 'Adolph? Sure, he's got his faults, but he's got some good points too,'" Erik says, then laughs.

I don't.

"You know, Princess, if I were a stand-up comedian and you were my audience, I'd be out of work, living in my car; hey, let's sit down in it if we're going to talk."

"Actually, I was thinking of talking in the quarry."

There. I've said it.

Erik looks more than surprised. He looks amazed. "The quarry? Now?"

I nod. "The quarry. Now."

He gives me another weird look. I smack my lips together and smile.

"Hey, sure. Sure, why not," he says and leads the way to his car. All the while, he's looking up and laughing, like he's sharing a silent joke with an invisible friend.

"This isn't about…you know…sex," I say, the last word coming out in a kind of whistled whisper.

"Of course it isn't," he says and laughs.

I'm not sure if he's agreeing with me or not, but I don't ask him for an explanation. In fact, I don't say anything for the rest of our walk. Neither does he. And once we're in Erik's car, the only sounds are from the engine and him lighting another cigarette. I roll down my window. At least he hasn't turned on the radio. I don't want a bunch of voices in my head. I need to stay focused.

"Don't bother lifting it," Erik says, as soon as we're parked in front of the quarry gate and he turns off his headlights. "Nobody can see us in the dark."

Did he *have* to say that?

After quietly closing the car doors, Erik takes my hand and we duck under the gate together. He leads the way down, still holding my hand. It's weird in the dark, but holding hands helps. So does having climbed down before.

At our clearing, Erik lets my hand drop.

"Okay, you want to talk here?" he says.

"On Sunwake."

"On Sunwake? Are you for real, girl?" Erik asks with a laugh. "I suppose you want us to swim there."

Chapter 12 - Quarry Starry Quarry

"I've got my bathing suit on, and I've got towels for both of us in my backpack."

"Princesssss!" Erik stretches the word way out. "You're really surprising me."

Two seconds later, his jeans and t-shirt are on the ground. He wears briefs, which I see for a second before he jumps in. I strip down to my bathing suit, and jump in too. Brrr…brrrr…what did I expect without the sun? *Never mind. Just swim, Jojo, swim.*

Erik's waiting up for me. We swim over to Sunwake together. He climbs on first, then reaches back to help me. There's no moon out tonight, so it's not very easy to see. I should have brought a flashlight.

"Your flower's still here," Erik says.

My eyes are still adjusting to the dark. Yes, there it is. I'd have felt crushed if it wasn't. I sit down next to it, and though I'd love to close my eyes, I don't. I know I've got to do this on my own, with just the quarry's magic to help me along. I wait for Erik to sit. He does so in the same spot as last time. It's chilly. Stupid me.

"So Marco took Harry and me to this island today, Bannerman's Arsenal," I say.

"Oh, yeah, I've been there."

I nod and look up. A few stars are twinkling in the sky. Maybe they've got planets, with people looking our way and wondering if the Sun has planets. Maybe those faraway planets have quarries on them, and wannabe writers. *Focus, Jojo, focus.*

"And Harry found a toy army tank there that made me realize we'll never change if we keep doing what we always do, like fight anyone we don't agree w-w-w-with—"

"Hey, you're shivering."

"I kn-kn-kn-know…" Stupid, stupid me.

"I should have realized you'd get cold. You're not the first person I've taken here at night." He stops and clears his throat.

"What's that supposed to mean?"

"Where do you think I got my nickname from? I'm the King of the Quarry. Here, let me warm you up."

He puts his arm around my shoulder. I can't help it. I shiver again, but it's a different type of shiver now. I can't get distracted. "Erik, can we get back to what I was trying to say."

"Sure, sure."

What just happened? It's like he changed the channel. He's not listening to me anymore. Where did he go? He squeezes me closer, which makes me warmer, yet I know to be on guard.

"So, burning down houses is a no-no according to the Princess. Well, make a better suggestion."

Does he have to sound so sarcastic?

"Maybe figure out how to stop kids from joining cults in the first place."

Chapter 12 - Quarry Starry Quarry

My body's vibrating. This isn't working. I've got no choice. I close my eyes.

Hello, flower, I practically scream in silence.

HELLO, JOLIE.

∽

It's Grandfatherly Figure. I'd hoped to see Erma. This is even better!

Did you know I'd come?

I KNOW YOU'RE MOVING ALONG RIGHT ON SCHEDULE.

I feel so strange, like my mind's expanding, I say, relieved to be honest, but that's not why I came back. But now that I'm here, I might as well tell him. *I took out a bunch of children's library books on astronomy so I could learn more about the universe. Does that make sense to you?*

Grandfatherly Figure nods. YOU ARE LEARNING WHAT YOU MUST AT A SAFE PACE. WE ARE VERY PLEASED. BUT YOU HAVE COME FOR A SPECIFIC PURPOSE TONIGHT AND YOU CAN'T STAY LONG, SO ASK YOUR QUESTION.

He knows! But of course he must.

I need help getting through to Erik, the guy who's with me. He wants to do something that's wrong, and I need to know how to stop him or else I need you to stop him. He's special to me.

YOUR FRIEND HAS MANY EXPERIENCES TO GO THROUGH AND LEARN FROM.

Quarry Face

But if you can stop him from hurting other people or himself, shouldn't you do it?

Grandfatherly Figure laughs a warm, kind laugh. *IN RETROSPECT, EVENTS WILL NOT SEEM AS CRUEL AS THEY MAY SEEM TODAY.*

How can that be?

When will retrospect come? I ask.

Grandfatherly Figure laughs his wonderful, full-bodied laugh again. I can't help trusting him, even if he doesn't give me straight answers. In fact, I trust him so much that I don't want to leave.

Can I stay here with you and Erma? This feels more like my home than anywhere else I've ever been, I say, although I expect I know the answer.

YOU WILL BE WITH US SOMEDAY. BUT FOR NOW, YOU, TOO, HAVE LESSONS TO LEARN.

Please let me stay, I say, surprised by my eagerness, and aware that my surroundings are even more physically barren than they were. Everything's meshed into a fuzzy halo of light, and Grandfatherly Figure himself is super fuzzy to me.

ERMA WILL BE PLEASED WITH HOW WELL YOU ARE DOING, he says, and with that he snaps his fingers.

Oh, no! No! Wait! Don't!

My eyes pop open. A wet tongue's on my lips.

Chapter 12 - Quarry Starry Quarry

"Erik, no, don't—" I push him away.

"That's not what the last girl I was here with said."

"Meaning?" I say, folding my arms over my chest. It's cold without Erik's arm around me.

"Let's just say, I've been here with other chicks and they were glad we didn't just talk."

This is no way for my future husband to act. Boy, does he have a lot of growing up to do.

"I'm sorry if you think I'm a freak," I say, and stand up. At least, here in the quarry, I know that no matter what he thinks of me, I'm fine the way I am.

"I can't figure you out. You're either the world's biggest tease or the most naïve girl on the planet."

"Most naïve, probably," I say, looking up. Somehow the stars are a comfort tonight. I don't know how to spot constellations, or which stars are which, but I feel watched and protected by them.

"We should go back," I say, and put out my hand to help him get up. "Don't worry, I won't bother you with this kind of stuff again. You can do whatever you want." I stop, surprised by how my voice cracked just then.

"Princess, you're too much," Erik replies.

Then he dives in, splashing me.

I was fine getting wet fast when we first came, probably because I thought more about my goal than about being cold, but it's chilly swimming back, following Erik. And once we're back on the shore, neither of us speak while we towel ourselves dry and get dressed, dry clothes over wet. I'll dash into the bedroom when I get home. I packed a baseball cap, which I'll put on as soon as I phone Marco.

~

We still haven't spoken when Erik drives up to Carmel Plaza, but I've got to break the silence now.

"Drop me off by The Video Palace. I'll phone Marco to get me."

"I can take you home."

"No, you shouldn't. I'd have too much explaining to do."

Erik nods. Seconds later, he's maneuvered into the parking spot we left and shuts off his ignition.

I can't help trying again. "I hope you don't go ahead with your plan, Erik."

He turns to me, "And I hope you think twenty times before you ask a guy over to your place or to the quarry at night. You're lucky I'm not a sex maniac or a serial killer. You're too trusting, Princess."

With that, he opens his door and slams it behind him, then walks all the way over to the curb before he stops.

I guess he's waiting for me.

Chapter 12 - Quarry Starry Quarry

And he's probably right. I shouldn't be so trusting. But I thought going to the quarry might help me get through to him or else Grandfatherly Figure or Erma might be willing to try. A tremble runs through me. Erik's lips on mine. His arm around my shoulder. No, no, no, I did not go to the quarry with ulterior motives. Or did I? How can I be sure? And how come I'm hearing that song from the movie *My Fair Lady* that Professor Higgins sings to Eliza Doolittle: "I've grown accustomed to her face, she almost makes the day begin…"

Martha's right. Erik would only hurt me if I fell in love with him.

He's still standing by the curb.

Might as well get out and phone for Marco to come get me. I'll try to fall asleep very quickly tonight, so I can wake up tomorrow with the energy I need to totally block Erik from my mind. And maybe Marco will take us back to the quarry, where I'll force myself to be satisfied with the confidence I gain there because I've pretty much been told there's no sense trying to return to Erma and Grandfatherly Figure.

I can't go home again. At least, not yet.

Chapter 13
Eve of Destruction

> Earth's pot is on the range,
> Spiced with new voices,
> Seasoned for change,
> And time-sensitive choices.
>
> Jolie Rich
> Carmel, New York

"Hi, sweetie. Did you have a good time?" Mom whispers, as Marco gently shuts the door behind us.

"Fine," I whisper back, sniffing. Popcorn?

"Well, I'm just glad you're home safe and sound. Marco? Hurry, it's almost over."

Marco moves around me to join Mom, who is sitting on the couch watching TV. He settles on the floor next to the coffee table. Mom points to the big bowl atop it.

"Stay, Jojo," she says. "Have some popcorn and when the movie ends, you can tell us what you did at The Video Palace."

Yeah, right.

Chapter 13 - Eve of Destruction

"Kids don't like giving reports," Marco says, looking up at me.

I must look surprised, because he laughs. "I was once your age, you know."

"So was I. It seems like just yesterday," Mom says. Then she laughs. "Actually, some days it seems more like a million years ago."

Uh oh. When she gets philosophical, it's time to go.

"Mom, I can hardly keep my eyes open," I say.

I hate lying. But my clothes feel clammy, and this isn't even my first lie of the day. Does it get easier to lie the older you get? But how can you always be honest? You hurt people or get in trouble or sound crazy if you are. It's a…stupid world. I wish it would change.

As soon as I flick on the light in my bedroom, I see *Childhood's End*. The book's on the floor by my bed. That's where I left it last night after rereading the ending: how the last man on Earth, a scientist, recorded what was happening as the planet dissolved. And afterwards, how the main Overlord, Karellen, looked back at the Solar System from far away, and could see the Sun, but couldn't tell that it had ever had planets orbiting it or that one of them was now gone.

It seemed so real.

Suddenly, a wail starts going nonstop outside. Wawa-wawa-wawa-wawa.

I quickly open my door.

Quarry Face

"What's going on?" I ask. It sounds like air-raid sirens from war movies.

Harry's wobbling out of Mom's bedroom, rubbing his eyes.

"Must be the fire siren," Marco tells us.

"Fire!" I cry.

"I'll phone the fire department and find out for sure," Marco says and heads for the kitchen.

He must have seen my face.

"Come, keep me company and tell me what you did tonight," Mom says, patting the couch on her left side.

That's where Erik patted when he was here. I don't move. In fact, I barely breathe as Harry plops down on Mom's right side and rests his head on her lap. I can hear Marco in the kitchen, voicing lots of 'uh huhs', and 'I sees.'

He returns to the living room. "The sirens summon volunteer firefighters to the firehouse. The guy I spoke to said the blaze is in a mansion at a place called Solomon Hill. Some self-proclaimed prophet's supposedly up there with his followers."

My knees cave. I've got to sit down, even if I am clammy. I sit as far from Mom and Harry as I can and ask, "Was anyone hurt?"

"They said it's a miracle nobody was," Marco replies.

Chapter 13 - Eve of Destruction

Oh, thank you, God, or luck, or whatever. But did Erik set the blaze? That's a very logical question, isn't it? He could have set it to start at a certain time and then gone to The Video Palace so he'd have an alibi. He could have known I was too late to stop him all along.

I stand up, a bit woozy. I touch my cap. Still on. I need to cry.

"Jojo? What's wrong, sweetie?"

I look at the floor so Mom can't see my eyes. Should I tell them about Erik's threat? What if it's just a big coincidence? I don't want to get him in trouble.

"Jojo? Did you hear me? Is something wrong?"

I shake my head and attempt a smile. But before I can say a word, truthful or not, the phone starts to ring.

Only one person calls this late.

I hurry back to my room.

∽

It's 3:11 a.m. according to my alarm clock, not that I understand time anymore—not since Sunwake; I don't get what it is. All I know is that it's not what it seems.

I had written in my journal before turning off my lamp around midnight. Then I heard Marco leave and Mom make up Harry's bed on the couch and wish him good night, so I've been lying here in the dark for three hours at least. Probably nobody else is still awake, and it's not that I don't want to sleep. But I can't stop thinking about Erik. Did he set the fire on Solomon Hill? How do I even think about stuff like that?

I reach for *Childhood's End* and clutch the book to my heart. Not that the Overlords can help by osmosis. And I'm nowhere near the quarry for any epiphany I might get from it, and even if I could talk to birds, I doubt they've got advice in human matters like these. I'm stalling. I know what I've got to do. Erik made a serious threat. I heard it. Dominick did too, but I doubt he'll snitch on his friend. No, it's up to me. But what if Erik's innocent? Maybe, by morning, the police will have found the real arsonist and it won't be Erik, just an amazing coincidence. That would be nice.

I very gently put *Childhood's End* back on the floor. Then I try once again to get comfortable in bed. This time I turn on my side and slip one hand under the pillow. The very next second, I'm throwing the soft, fuzzy lump I felt so hard that it hits the wall. Two seconds later, I'm scooping up the poor stuffed frog and bringing it back to bed. It's not the frog's fault that Erik's an idiot.

I've got no choice. Tomorrow morning I've got to tell Marco what Erik said. Yes, it should be Marco, not Mom. She'd get all upset and then we'd *both* need Marco. I'm sure he'll be more rational than her about whether I should go to the police. I wish I'd never heard Erik's threat. You stupid human being, you, even if you are cute with that floppy hair of yours and that Ringo Starr kind of sneer, like everything's a big joke. Well, it's not—not when other people are concerned.

I turn on my side and shut my eyes again. I need energy for tomorrow. I must get to sleep. Get to sleep? That sounds odd now, like sleep's a place you journey

Chapter 13 - Eve of Destruction

to. Oh, this is nice. I'm heading for the quarry in my mind, walking down the hill and looking at that circle of tadpoles I saw in my dream the other night, and now there are frogs, yes frogs, coming down the hill, lots of frogs from every direction. I'm still human, but then, this is only a dream, and in it I'm stopping to take a deep breath and look into the distance. Oh, no! Huge yellowish-red flames are piercing the sky all around us, but I'm the only one who sees them and knows they're coming our way!

I must warn everyone!

But where can we go?

I bolt up in bed. This is not funny! How can I fall asleep if I'm worried about saving all the *frogs* in the quarry? They're just frogs, but I feel responsible for them. Is this what it's like to go crazy? Your dreams take over your waking life?

JUST GET THROUGH TONIGHT, MY DEAR. THE TRUTH WILL SOON BE CRYSTAL CLEAR.

My head crashes back down on my pillow. Was that Grandfatherly Figure in my mind, or my own thought? How can I tell? For that matter, how can I know anything for sure? It's not that I feel stupid, like when Dad yells at me. It's more like, at this moment, I feel wise enough to know how little I know.

All of a sudden, I'm feeling super tired. Here I go again, turning on my side, slipping one hand under my pillow. Erik's frog is now on the floor, next to *Childhood's End*. My hand feels good sandwiched between the cool pillowcase and sheet and I'm heading for dreamland,

Quarry Face

back to the quarry, while flames all around still rage and roar, yet something's changed. Now I know to have no fear, plus far, far more than I ever dreamt I'd know before.

Chapter 14
Welcome To Carmel

> Tomorrow's Creator,
> A tight schedule to keep,
> Guides travelers with waves
> Multi-layered and deep.
>   Jolie Rich
>   Carmel, New York

"Hi!" I shout, as Marco's kitchen screen door slams behind me.

Didn't mean to do that. But nobody's in the kitchen, anyway. The 1985 Ace Hardware calendar hanging on the wall has a big red X on every day in August up until today, Saturday the 17th. I'll be glad when it's the 18th and today's behind me.

"We're up here," Marco shouts down.

Hmm. Sheets and a pillow on the couch. Makes sense. I had passed a second car in Marco's driveway. Probably not Mira, though, not if his guest slept downstairs.

I run up all the stairs until, at the top, I blink my eyes and shriek, "Marco, is that you?"

"You like it?" he asks, standing by the banister, stroking his clean-shaven face.

He looks much younger, like a teenager really.

"I like you much better without a beard," I confess.

"Me, too," chimes a woman's voice.

I turn towards Marco's bedroom. Her curly brown hair is longer than in Marco's slides of Paris, but I know exactly who it is. "I was hoping you'd come. You're Mira!"

"And you're Jolie. I've heard a lot about you."

"I've heard about you, too," I say, my smile growing.

I walk over to where she's sitting with Harry on Marco's bed and hand over *Childhood's End*. "I was returning this to Marco. You're the one who said I should read it."

"Can you guys continue this at the quarry?" Marco asks as he snaps a photo of Mira, Harry, and me.

Mira raises her hand, like he should stop shooting. Then she looks up at me. "I wanted to see the quarry before I leave. I've got to fly out tonight. I'm going where your aunt is, Jolie—to Medjugorje."

"You're kidding!" I exclaim. "So, do you know what's really going on there?"

"Well…" Mira begins.

"Oh, no you don't," Marco interrupts, sitting down next to Mira and putting his arm around her shoulder. "Honey,

Chapter 14 - Welcome To Carmel

you've got to continue this at the quarry. You're running out of time."

Mira looks up at me, smiles, and takes one of my hands in hers.

"Come with us. We can talk while we're there," she says.

I've got so many questions to ask. About my boulder. About *Childhood's End*. And now about Medjugorje, too. About how come she slept on the couch. I guess that's a question I shouldn't ask.

But how come?

"You may never get another chance like this," Marco says.

He's being funny, but maybe it's true. Oh, what should I do? I wanted to tell him about Erik, but not in front of Mira. If Erik turns out to be innocent, the fewer people who hear my suspicions, the better. But if he's guilty, he should be turned in.

Marco's looking at me. His eyes are bloodshot, like I'm not the only one who didn't sleep much last night. How can I not go to the quarry if Mira asks me to? Maybe I'll take Marco aside and talk to him there. And maybe I can go to Sunwake with Mira, and be honest with her about what happened to me on it.

"Okay, I'll go," I say, before asking, "Marco, did you hear anything more about that fire?"

Marco shakes his head.

Quarry Face

"But everything seems under control," he says and drops a lens into his camera case. "So let's get this show on the road."

I turn to Harry. "Race you home—"

Before I can say another word, Harry's dashed down the stairs.

By the time I get outside, my brother's way over on the other side of the bushes. Did I do right, not talking to Marco? I swear, boys can really mess up your thinking. When I reach the cottage, just before I open the front door, I turn back. Marco and Mira are standing at Marco's bedroom window, watching me. His arm's around her shoulder. I wave. They wave back.

So, what's their story?

Oh look. There's a bird pecking at some of Aunt Tish's squash. That should keep him busy for a while.

But there's no time for Test #130 now.

Chapter 15
No Trespassing, Take Two

> *Wipe your mind,*
> *Lest negativity lurks*
> *And mars tomorrow*
> *With ancient quirks.*
>   Jolie Rich
>   Carmel, New York

Marco and Mira seem almost giddy in the car, the way they jump from one subject to another, talking about friends and relatives, and Mira's upcoming trip, and then that terrible plane crash last week in Japan.

"Five hundred people died. Their poor families. I wish air travel were safer. Better yet, why can't someone invent teleportation?"

"Yeah, why not," I echo from the back seat. I totally agree with Mira.

"Never happen," Marco says.

"Mr. Never Happen," Mira calls him as she playfully punches his arm. "If humans used their intelligence to work together on scientific breakthroughs instead of all the other crap they focus on, innovations like that would come a lot sooner."

"Yeah," I agree again.

Marco doesn't reply. He keeps looking straight ahead as he makes that last turn before the quarry's gate. Then he idles his motor. The Keep Out sign is still here. Oh well.

"Time to do your thing," he says.

The rest of us get out. Harry and I head for one side of the gate and Mira heads for the other. From there, she yells, "You guys ever worry about getting caught?"

"All the time!" I admit.

"Really?" Marco sounds surprised, as if I never said I did.

"Marco will protect us. He said so. Right Marco?" Harry shouts.

Marco nods, a broad smile on his face, as Mira tells us to lift the chain on her count of three. It works like a charm. Soon Marco's driving through and honking his horn.

Oh, must he?

"No, Marco," I mouth, so he won't honk again. He's probably showing off for Mira, but what if the owner hears? Or Erik, who's hiding in the bushes, waiting to drown me because I know too much. I can't help thinking that. Maybe I've seen too many crime shows on TV.

Chapter 15 - No Trespassing, Take Two

I let Mira go ahead of me. The guys are already halfway down. They've got the floats and pump, but Harry's water wings are in my backpack, so no matter how fast they run, they'll still have to wait for us.

"How did you get so strong? I can't lift the chain by myself." I yell down to Mira.

"Years of practice," she says, glancing back over her shoulder. "So, Marco says you're a big thinker."

It's weird to know people talk about you when you're not around.

"Yeah, I guess I think a lot. Probably too much," I say, raising my voice because she's facing front again.

"Some people are born to think," she replies.

It's like being struck by lightning. She's right! I *was* born to think. Whoops. Better watch where I'm going. No time to think now. By the time we reach the clearing, the guys have the red float inflated and are working on the blue.

"Boy, you're fast," Mira tells Marco.

"Harry's help is the secret," he replies.

My brother grins from ear to ear. I look around. No sign of Erik, but if he was sneaky enough to start the fire yesterday, he could be here, hiding somewhere. It takes will power not to think about him as I take off my t-shirt and watch the guys finish inflating the second float. When they're done, Marco takes some shots of me and Mira. She's got on a one-piece bathing suit, and she's laughing, like she thinks Marco's obsession with photography is cute. He's using more lenses than he usually does. When he's done, he puts his camera back into his case, and has Harry throw the floats into the water. Then, holding their noses, he and Harry jump in together.

Mira's next.

I want to always remember this moment with the four of us in the quarry. My eyes are getting watery. Damn that Erik. Thinking about him ruins everything.

"The water's wonderful, just like I remember," Mira says, swimming over with the red float to where I'm standing.

I jump in like I did last night.

"Brrr," I say and give myself a wet hug. Was I really here just hours ago?

"Kick your feet to get warm," Mira tells me.

Soon we're both holding on to the float and kicking, and I'm warmer, but—

"Is something wrong?" Mira asks.

I immediately nod and shake my head so vigorously that we both laugh.

"I'd rather not say," I admit, and Mira nods, like she's not going to pressure me into talking. Anyway, I don't feel as bad as I thought I would. The quarry's magic must be doing its thing.

Chapter 15 - No Trespassing, Take Two

Suddenly, Mira points left and says, "Look, Jolie! See the boulder with the white flower? That's where we're going. That's the spot Marco said you like. Right?"

Oh, very, very right. "I call it Sunwake."

"Sunwake? Great name," Mira says, as we kick our way towards it.

Mira steps onto the boulder first, then stretches out her hand to grab mine. Once I'm up beside her, we pull the float out of the water and wedge it safely in a crevice. Then we sit on opposite sides of the flower, like I did with the boy whose name I want out of my head except for when I tell Marco about his threat.

But Mira might find this interesting.

"I told a boy I was here with, that whatever he wished would come true if he kissed the flower."

"Did he make a wish?"

"Marco started taking photos of us just then, so he never got a chance!"

"That Marco!" Mira says, like she's exasperated, but I can tell she loves him.

It feels good to laugh with Mira, to be with her here.

"What about you? Did you make a wish?" she asks.

I can see the guys across the quarry. Looks like Harry's having fun.

Quarry Face

"I did, but you may laugh if I tell it to you."

"You should try me."

"I wished for peace. Peace on Earth and peace in our universe."

Mira pulls her knees up to her chest. Then she smiles and says, "In Medjugorje, the Virgin Mary tells the kids that peace starts within one's heart."

"But do you believe the Virgin Mary is really appearing there? I can't get myself to believe in miracles," I say. A second later I snort a laugh. What do I call meeting blobs that turn into human forms right inside my mind? Why can't I call that a miracle?

"Marco said you two talked about *Childhood's End*," Mira says.

She's changed the subject, but that's okay. There's so much I want to talk to her about. "I loved the book, except I thought it was old-fashioned, and it made me sad at the end because Earth got destroyed, even if I understood it had to happen. I know it wasn't because people were bad, as much as it was just the natural progression of things. Still, I kept hoping the planet could be saved. But did you love the book too?"

"It meant a lot to me. Arthur C. Clarke is a visionary."

A shiver runs through me. I'm about to ask, "Does that mean it's true that Earth will be destroyed?" when I see she's closed her eyes. I know Grandfatherly Figure and Erma don't want me back yet, but if she's doing that, maybe—

Chapter 15 - No Trespassing, Take Two

Without saying another word out loud, I draw my knees up to my chest and close my eyes too. Everything's dark here, while the sun's shimmering on the other side of my eyelids.

Hi, flower, I say silently, just in case I should. *I'm back.*

∽

I don't recognize where I am anymore. What I see is formless now, as if I was just in a stage setting before, like the castle on Bannerman's Arsenal. Yet I know I'm in the right place because I feel I'm home again and look— there's Erma!

Hi, I say in my silent voice.

She's running towards me, her face glowing.

Mira and Jolie. I'm so glad you're here together!

I do a quarter turn. I pinch myself. It hurts.

Do you know what's going on? I ask Mira, because she's beside me, as clearly as she's sitting with me on a boulder in the quarry.

I know some answers, Mira says inside my head and motions for me to move along with her and Erma. *I thought you might be one of us, but I wasn't 100% sure until now.*

One of us? Us what? And where are we? Everyone speaks in riddles here. Suddenly I panic. *Where's the man you were with? Is he your grandfather? Is he…?"*

He's everyone's grandfather! And he's very, very busy. But he sends his love.

Quarry Face

Good. He's not dead, although like time, I suspect dead doesn't mean what I grew up thinking it did. Erma's words, 'his love,' shower me with feeling, but I want to see him again and not just hear his words passed on. I run my fingers along Sunwake's stone surface. I can feel the heat and the water on the rock. No, this isn't a dream. This is real.

Jolie, it's too early for you to understand what's happening," Mira's words cut into my thoughts. *"But it's important to know that what you feel is real. You're lucky. I had nobody on Earth to share my experiences with when I was your age.*

But can't I know more now? I ask. *I've already been here twice before. Ask Erma.* Saying her name makes me vibrate.

Mira turns to Erma, *Does that mean she's ready to learn about the transition?*

Transition? What transition? I ask. More riddles.

Erma glances around. Then she gives a gigantic shrug and says, **Give it a try.**

Mira clears her voice.

Suddenly, I'm scared. I don't want to hear anything frightening. Meanwhile, we're all three moving in sync, me and Mira and a blob turned into a child. Weird, no?

Still walking, Mira looks at me and says, *You're very special, Jolie. You belong to a generation born to begin a transition to a new reality—*

"Hey, get out of there! You hear me! Get out of there!"

Chapter 15 - No Trespassing, Take Two

My eyes flash open. Who's shouting?

"Mira! Jolie! Start back!" Marco's yelling, his voice cracking.

I can't see him or anyone else from here, but my stomach's knotting.

"We'd better go," Mira says, standing up.

She tosses our float into the water, then jumps in and grabs hold of it. Now she's waiting for me.

I can't go without kissing my flower. *I wish for peace everywhere in our universe.*

Okay, now I'm ready, I guess. I hope this doesn't mean no more quarry. That would be impossible, wouldn't it?

The voices grow louder and louder the nearer we get to the clearing. There's barking, too. Closer still, and I can see that Marco's got one arm around Harry and is gesturing with the other. Two men are with them. The older one's shouting. He's got a dog, a big black dog on a leash. I think it's a Doberman.

The younger guy's in his twenties, I guess. He's not saying a peep.

He's holding a rifle.

Chapter 16
A Matter of Time

> Words are precious,
> Like water and air;
> Use them to unite,
> Not con, hurt, or scare.
> Jolie Rich
> Carmel, New York

The rifle's pointing down, but still, it's a rifle. Rifles can kill.

"Down boy, down!" the old man's yelling as Marco helps me and Mira out of the water. I rush over to the rock where I left my sunglasses and grab them. The dog's still barking, but his tail's wagging. I don't trust barking dogs, period. I don't think Harry does, either. He's gripping Marco's waist.

"This property's private. You think I put that sign up as a joke?" The old man's shouting, his face getting redder and redder.

The dog growls, his tail still wagging.

"Well, it's a great swimming hole—"

Chapter 16 - A Matter of Time

"Don't 'great-swimming-hole' *me,* you damn hippies!" the man shouts before Marco can finish. "I'm the one who's got to worry about insurance. If one of you jerks breaks a neck here, who do you think pays? I do. Not you. We knew there were people swimming here, so just consider yourself lucky, until today. Now we got your license plate number, so don't come sneaking back, you hear? Next time I call the cops."

The younger guy motions with the rifle for us to head up the hill.

We quickly gather our stuff, while the old guy rattles on about us showing no respect for the law. "Selfish, that's all you are. Selfish hippies…" he keeps muttering as Marco nods for us to go ahead of him.

I push Harry up the hill first. Mira's behind me, and Marco's in the rear. We're carrying our clothes and towels, the floats and air pump, and Marco's got his camera case, too. The owner is following behind us, mumbling about how no good we are. The one time I dare look back, the younger guy has his hand on the old guy's back, like he's helping him walk. Meanwhile, the dog keeps growling and wagging its tail as it runs up alongside us.

"You doing okay?" Mira asks me as we near the top.

I'm walking as fast as I can in unlaced sneakers and with the red float balanced on both our heads.

"Super," I reply, my eyes watery. Marco shouldn't have honked.

In the meanwhile, the old guy keeps warning us he'll call the cops if we return.

Quarry Face

Marco keeps repeating, "Don't worry, we're not coming back," right until we reach the Volvo. He hustles me and Harry into the back seat. Then he shoves the inflated floats over our laps, letting them stick out both side windows.

"Hey, Pops, relax. You know how much Mom worries about your angina when you get all riled up. Besides, you made your point," the son says as he unlocks the metal chain gate. "They're leaving."

No more quarry. I look out the back window. This feels like the end of the world, like how that last guy must have felt in *Childhood's End*. Okay, maybe I'm being a bit dramatic... but not really. I can't bear the thought of writing about today. It's too sad.

As soon as I turn around to the front again, Marco says, "Cheer up, Jolie. You can still see the quarry in my slides."

He's watching me in his rearview mirror.

"I know." I don't want him to feel bad, but I can't imagine a photo, even one Marco takes, that would make me feel like I did there.

"Aw, don't cry, Jojo," Harry says, putting his arm around my shoulder.

A weepy laugh escapes me. I hope my brother always stays this sweet.

"I'm glad we got a chance to spend some time together in the quarry," Mira says, reaching back to give my knee a pat. "I guess I wasn't meant to say as much as I thought I could."

Marco gives Mira a weird look.

Chapter 16 - A Matter of Time

"Oh, Marco, I know you don't believe I'm being guided, but I love you just the same," she says and leans over to kiss him on the cheek.

Guided? I want to ask what she means, but Marco's shaking his head, so I figure I better not. Instead, I pretty much say nothing all the way back. Nobody else is talking, either, until Marco turns into his driveway.

"Let's have lunch together before I go," Mira says. "Okay, Marco? Okay, kids?"

We all nod. Good, because I've got to talk to Mira before she goes. There's so much still to ask.

Suddenly, she snaps her fingers. "I just remembered. We're out of milk. We finished it with our coffee this morning."

"I'll bring some over from our place," I volunteer. Anyway, I want a few minutes alone for a quick cry.

The instant we've got the floats off our legs, I'm out of the car, dashing towards the cottage. I feel like I can't wait to let it all out, to cry and scream. It's like I've lost my home, my family, my confidence, and hope.

As I break through the bushes, my heart starts racing, and my feet tremble so that I nearly trip in front of the person waiting for me.

Erik!

Chapter 17
Arrow of Time

> There's no going back
> Once you're on your way,
> Lest you miss your date
> At the cosmic café.
>   Jolie Rich
>   Carmel, New York

Erik's sitting on Aunt Tish's stoop, shoulders slumped, head down. Maybe I should run and get Marco. Erik's looking up now and starts to stand. I keep walking closer, passing our garden of squash, and not stopping until I look straight into his face. His eyes are as bloodshot as mine and Marco's.

"You just get back from the quarry?" he asks.

"We were officially kicked out today."

"You were what?" He does a double take. Then he clears his voice, and narrowing those bloodshot eyes, asks, "Did you say kicked out?"

I nod. It's not easy holding back tears, but I do. I don't think I could stand breaking down in front of Erik and

Chapter 17 - Arrow of Time

having him think me a crybaby. "We got chased out by two guys, a father and son. The son had a rifle."

"A rifle? No kidding?"

I can't help sniffling as I nod again. "A real rifle, and they had a big black dog that kept barking and wagging its tail. The older guy said if we ever come back, he'll call the cops."

"That bum. I should kill him!" Erik says, holding out a fist.

"Kill him?"

"No, Jesus, not *really* kill him. Look, I came by to tell you that I may have *said* I'd burn down Joy Star's mansion, but I sure as hell didn't mean it. I was *teasing* you. I'm a big tease. Everyone knows that. And sometimes I can be cruel and play games. Okay? I admit it. I'll even go to confession and tell Father Padilla I lied. Now are you happy?"

Father Padilla must be Erik's priest. Still, you shouldn't joke around about stuff like arson.

"So, the fire last night was just a big coincidence?"

"Hell yes. I may be a liar and a tease—"

"And a big bully."

"Okay, *and* a big bully, but I don't set fires, except maybe in fireplaces," he says with a laugh. "And grills."

I refuse to laugh.

He cuts short his own laughter. "You believe me, don't you?"

"I'm not sure."

"C'mon, believe me! First of all, I've got witnesses who were with me every minute last night until I went home, and my mom can vouch for me there. Wait a minute, you're not going to deny being together in the quarry, are you?"

"My mom will kill me if she ever finds out."

Erik laughs and looks up toward the sky. "That's a good one. I give the girl a dilemma right from the start." He turns back to face me. "Look, Princess, whether you believe me or not, I learned my lesson. I couldn't sleep all night worrying you'd tell someone my threat, and I'd wind up getting blamed for every unsolved fire in New York State. I thought of phoning you to try to explain, but I worried that might make you even more suspicious. What a stupid, idiotic night."

"You can say that again," I say.

"From the start? Or just the part about the stupid night?"

I shrug. How can I ever trust him now that I know he lies?

He's narrowing his eyes again. "Hey, you didn't tell anyone, did you?"

"I was going to tell Marco, but then his girlfriend showed up, and I didn't want to say anything with her

Chapter 17 - Arrow of Time

around, in case I was wrong. I figured I should just tell him, and he'd help me figure out whether to go to the police or—"

"Good reasoning," Erik says, like he's surprised it's mine. Then he looks up at the sky again and says, "Thank You, Guys, for small favors."

Guys? What's that mean? I know it's not Grandfatherly Figure and Erma. Not the Overlords, either, because they're not real. And not the Virgin Mary, because he's saying 'Guys,' not 'Gal.'

"I'm serious, Princess," he says, looking back at me. "I won't go through this hell twice. I bet it aged me 30 years. I'm through being a tease. Well, at least I'll try not to be. So, c'mon, let's make up and be friends."

He whips out a white paper bag. That explains why he only made one fist.

"What is it?" I ask, as he puts the bag under my nose. I think I know.

"It's a peace offering—chocolate chip cookies from my mom's favorite bakery. I would have liked some with walnuts, but you can't have everything. So, we made up this morning, my mom and me. I said I'm fine with her dating Big Al. And we had a big cry together."

He stops and looks down, then starts to smile and faces me again. "He really does bake the best chocolate chip cookies you've ever had. So, what do you say? Can we be friends and share a cookie?"

He's sounding cuter and cuter. But I remember Martha's warning. Guys like Erik are dangerous because they make you want to believe they're sincere.

"I'm not sure I want to be your friend," I say.

"We've got something in common. I don't want to be my friend, either. C'mon, Princess. I'll turn over a new leaf. Okay, how about a whole tree?"

I'm standing here in Carmel, but suddenly in my mind I'm back in my vice principal's office a few months ago. He's congratulating me on being salutatorian because of my consistently high grades, and for an instant, I'm thinking Elyse gets all the breaks, so I won't tell him her grades are higher. Then the instant passes and I tell the truth and, of course, he doesn't believe me anyway!

The point is, I almost lied. The thought crossed my mind.

"I guess none of us are perfect," I say.

"You can say that again." Erik replies. Then he makes an exaggerated cough, pounds his chest with his fist, and starts reaching for his cigarettes.

"I wish you'd stop smoking."

"Hey, I said 'let's make up,' not 'let's make me over,'" Erik says.

"Jojo! We're waiting for the malk!" Harry yells, waving to us from the bushes.

I wave back.

Chapter 17 - Arrow of Time

"Hurry!" he shouts before vanishing.

Erik blows out his match, then repeats, "Malk?"

"Mom told me I used to say malk instead of milk, just like him, when I was his age. She said she did, too, like it's genetic."

Invite Erik to lunch.

"You should stay and have lunch with us," I say, surprised by my thought. Was it mine or—?

"Why? You call the cops and they said to stall me if I showed up?"

"No, but I'll remember that for next time," I say, unable to squelch my smile.

"There won't be a next time," Erik mutters. "I've learned my lesson. So, you're really inviting me to stay?"

I nod, my hand on the doorknob.

"Okay, sure. Why not? It's a free lunch, right?" he says, as he takes a drag and starts to follow me inside.

"A free lunch," I repeat. But—and please don't ask how I know this because I can't say—I've got a feeling Erik's due for a lot more than a free lunch today.

Maybe I am, too.

Chapter 18
Last Launch

> *On the right wavelength,*
> *The gates open wide*
> *For those moving on*
> *With truth at their side.*
> Jolie Rich
> Carmel, New York

"It's not funny!" I say, as Marco performs his charade of the father, the son, and the dog kicking us out of the quarry. Everyone else here in Marco's living room is laughing, especially when he goes *arf, arf* for the Doberman. I don't get it. I thought Mira would be much sadder. And I was sure Erik would stay upset. Instead, he's standing by Marco's fireplace, laughing his head off and looking totally innocent.

At first, Dad swore he never slept with his secretary. *She* was the one who told Mom the truth. Then he confessed everything. And now he's trying to win Mom back, phoning her every night. I don't understand how you can ever again trust anyone you catch in a gigantic lie, especially one that he's got to know will hurt you.

Marco runs in place to imitate us racing up the hill. Then he bows.

Chapter 18 - Last Launch

"You were great," Mira says and applauds, like the rest of us do. Then she reaches over to Marco's coffee table for the cookies I had Erik bring. Two bites and she's beaming.

"This is the best chocolate chip cookie I've ever had," she says. "Is the bakery in Carmel?"

"Brewster. Erik's mom's new boyfriend baked them," I reply.

Erik frowns. Did I say something wrong?

"So you both live in Carmel?" he asks, pointing from Mira to Marco.

Marco sits down in his rocking chair as Mira responds. "Marco's up here most weekends. Otherwise, he's at our— *his* apartment in Manhattan. I'm here to say goodbye before I leave for Medjugorje. That's a small town in—"

"Yugoslavia! I know where Medjugorje is!" Erik exclaims, waving his cheese sandwich. "My mom's priest is taking a church group there in December. I just read about it yesterday while I was..." he stops to clear his throat. "My mom keeps her church newsletters in a basket in our bathroom. She knows that's the only place I'll ever read them."

We all laugh. Marco's glancing at his wristwatch. Not yet, please, not yet.

Erik goes on, "I read that some kids there claim they've been seeing the Virgin Mary and getting messages from her every day since June 24th, 1981. I know the exact day her visits started, because June 24th is my mom's birthday. If I miss it, I'm toast. But I find the whole Medjugorje thing a bit hard to believe. I mean, this is the 20th century. If I were the Virgin Mary, why would I appear to just a few kids in a tiny village? Why not go on television and get seen by millions of people at once? It doesn't make sense to me."

Good point.

"The reason's not ours to know," Mira says.

"Okay, so why are *you* going?" Erik asks. "Are you looking for some kind of a cure? That's why most of my mom's friends signed up. And my mom says being there might help her get over my dad's death."

Brinnnng, brinnnnng, brinnnnng.

"Saved by the bell. It's probably my sister, Anna," Marco says, grabbing his sandwich and rushing towards the stairs. "I'll bring down my latest slides of the quarry when I'm done."

None of us say a word until we hear Marco start to talk on his phone upstairs. That's when Erik leans over towards Mira and in a stage whisper says, "Okay, now let's hear the real story. You're running off to Medjugorje to meet your secret lover, right?"

Erik's grinning, like he's being funny, but that's what I wondered, too! It's a shame to think stuff like that. I look down at Harry, who's munching his second cookie, and humming to himself like he's in his own private world. I used to pretend to be like that at his age so adults wouldn't think I was listening to things I knew they didn't want me to hear.

Chapter 18 - Last Launch

"I'm traveling alone, but I always feel guided," Mira tells Erik.

"Hah! You should shake hands with my friend, Jimbo," Erik immediately responds. "He thought he was guided, too: guided to run off and join that screwball, Joy Star. And guess what?" Erik's gaze goes from Mira to me. "This morning my friend, Bobby, called to say Jimbo's back home. He's convinced that the fire on Solomon Hill was God's warning that he'd burn in hell if he didn't beat it out of there fast."

"So, now he's safe, except from me, because I'm going to wring his neck for running off like that. But what I'm getting at is that he claimed to feel guided, just like you say you are," continues Erik, taking a deep breath. "No offense, but people who say they're guided are just making excuses for doing what they want to do in the first place, or else they're brainwashed or crazy. I don't trust any of them."

"It's good to be skeptical," Mira replies. "Frankly, I'm a bit confused myself right now. I thought I was guided to talk to Jolie, but I hardly began when we got kicked out of the quarry."

"Coincidence," Erik mumbles.

"I suppose," Mira replies.

She sounds to me like she doesn't mean that.

For a few minutes, all I hear is Marco laughing upstairs, and Harry down here singing "The Itsy Bitsy Spider" while he makes a tiny hill on his paper plate from everyone's cookie crumbs.

Quarry Face

Read the letter.

There it is again, that voice in my head that I don't think is mine, the one that told me to invite Erik over.

Marco's not here. Shouldn't I wait for him?

Read it now.

~

"I just got a letter from Aunt Tish in Medjugorje," I say, standing up and reaching into the pocket of the pants I had changed into before Erik and I headed over here. We passed the mailman just as he drove away.

"Yay! A letter from Aunt Tish!" Harry shouts.

"Maybe we should wait for—" Mira points upstairs.

I shake my head. She nods, as I carefully open the envelope.

"I better skim it first," I say.

Erik laughs. "Keep us in suspense."

"No, it's because Aunt Tish has terrible handwriting. I don't want to trip over her words," I explain. But to my surprise, her writing's legible. She never wrote this neat before, not on greeting cards or postcards or the scrawling house-sitting notes she left for us up here. I give it a quick scan. It's enough to have me grinning as I clear my throat and begin.

Chapter 18 - Last Launch

"My Dearest Sister, Jolie, and Harry,

Hi! Still here in Medjugorje, but leaving on the 20th. It's been amazing! We've been videotaping the kids, who seem very sincere. And it's been wonderful interviewing visitors from around the world about the miracles they claim to have experienced. Truth or fiction? Can't say, but we've got great footage. And guess what? Sit down for this..."

I pause and sit back down on the couch. Harry giggles. I go on.

"It's really major! One night, after filming all day, we were looking up at the sky, when Chuck suddenly said, 'Love is all that really matters, isn't it?' So I said, 'I guess so.' And the next thing he said was, 'Okay, I'm ready. Should I get down on my knee?' And then he asked me to marry him. Isn't that great! Hope your summer's going well. See you soon.

Love, Sis & Aunt Tish

P.S. Hope you guys didn't plant all that squash. After meeting some farmers here, I realize how fast it grows! I wonder if I'll get any hybrids this year. If not, there's always next!"

"Can I go to the wedding?" Harry asks, as soon as I put the letter down.

"Of course," I tell him.

"Oh, goody!" he says and claps. He looks so happy!

I can't say the same for Erik.

"I'm sorry," he says, vigorously shaking his head. "My mom might believe what's going on in Medjugorje, but I've got to see my own proof to believe anything. There are too many people running around claiming to, quote, 'know the real truth,' unquote, for me to believe any of them."

"I agree," Mira tells him. "But I got my proof. Too bad I can't simply pass it on to you."

"And what kind of proof was that?" Erik asks.

Good question. I'd like to know, too.

"It's something that happened to me in the quarry, on one of the boulders in there."

"Sunwake?" I whisper.

When Mira nods, I feel like my heart's stopped beating.

"So, what happened?" Erik asks, glancing at me, then back at Mira.

He's smirking, like he doesn't expect to be convinced by anything she says.

Mira looks at us like she's not sure if she should go on.

"Please…" I say. I want to hear her proof. I *need* to hear her proof.

Harry's laughing because I'm clasping my hands just like he does when he wants something real bad.

Mira nods at me, takes a deep breath and says, "When I was younger, about Jolie's age, my parents had good

Chapter 18 - Last Launch

friends with a summer place up here. We visited them on weekends, and during one visit, we discovered the quarry. None of the adults took the Keep Out sign seriously. They assumed the place belonged to a mining company that had forgotten about it. I loved swimming there. It felt wonderful to me. "Like magic," I used to say. Somehow, the guys with us—my father, his friends, their sons—didn't feel the same way, but other females did. And one day I swam over to the boulder in the quarry that Jolie calls Sunwake, and my life changed forever."

Mira pauses. Now she's looking from me to Erik and back again as if she's not sure she should say more.

"Please…" I hope she can tell how much her story means to me.

She starts talking again, but slower, as if she's weighing every word.

"I can't go into details, and they won't mean much to you at this point anyway," she says, directing her response to Erik. Then she turns to me, "What matters is that I *knew* from my experience that there's more to life than we know, and that I had to work on myself so I'd be ready years from then when people began waking up to a shift in reality. I was given a glimpse of the future and told to keep it a secret until signs started to appear."

"What kind of signs?" I ask.

"I don't know for sure, just that they'll be unmistakable," Mira replies. "Maybe they'll be books or magazine articles or movies or TV shows that resonate with a new kind of energy. Or maybe they'll be revealed in world events or in dreams, whether collectively shared or dreamt by one or a few trusted individuals. However they come, the signs will be a clear wake-up call for those destined to move on to seek out guides and fellow travelers, and to review their lives with a new eye, an eye on evolving their cosmic consciousness."

Mira stops and smiles, "That's a surprise. I didn't think I'd get all of that out."

I've got a ton of questions, but silence seems best right now. Erik's not speaking either. Harry's trying to sneak a cookie into his lap. For a while, all we hear is Marco upstairs, laughing.

Then Mira speaks again. "I expect a transition period in which some people will bring history to a close, while others of all ages, religions, nationalities, and sexes, will consciously move in the direction they've been subconsciously moving in since birth."

Now she's looking straight at me. "It has to do with energy, being allowed to receive and shape a powerful energy for the good of the universe. You understand, Jolie, don't you?"

"I think so," I reply. "But did you get back to Sunwake a lot?" That's my not-so-subtle way of finding out how often she visited Grandfatherly Figure and Erma.

Mira closes her eyes. "Yes, I got back several times that summer I was fifteen, but I pretty much was told to stay away after my first encounter," Mira laughs. "I came to accept that I'd been privileged—whether by destiny or by being in the right energy spot at the right time—to learn what I did. Since then, I've been trying to be the best I can be in everything I do. It's not easy. And I keep hoping signs

Chapter 18 - Last Launch

will come, so I can share my secrets. When Marco found this house to rent, I thought that might be a sign. But I've been back to…Sunwake…and it was always just another boulder. Nothing special. Until today. With Jolie."

She opens her eyes and looks at me, "Yet we got kicked out, which I take to mean we've still got a ways to go."

"What about Medjugorje? Is *that* a sign?" Erik asks.

"I play the role of journalist, Erik. I write articles about interesting people and places that I assume I'm being guided to. And right now I'm drawn to Medjugorje, so I'll go there, write about it, and at the same time, keep a low profile. That's for my own protection."

Erik laughs, a kind of delirious laugh, if you ask me.

"Where the hell are you from, lady? Venus or Transylvania?" he asks.

"Maybe I've said too much," Mira replies. "But if so, you'll forget what you've heard, or you won't take me seriously. That's how it works. Knowledge and energy are protected."

Mira stops talking again. As I watch her, *Childhood's End* pops into my head— Karellen silently bidding farewell to the generations he'd known on Earth as he swiftly travels away from the Solar System, in which Earth orbits no more.

"I—" I begin, but Erik's voice drowns me out.

"Just so you know, last night before that fire at Joy Star's mansion, I told Jolie I wanted to burn it down. Really. That's what I said, not that I'd ever really do it. I'd be crazy to risk jail for something stupid like that. I was just teasing Jolie because she's so gullible and, oh—I don't know—maybe I thought I could talk her into doing something she wouldn't otherwise, just so she could save Joy Star's skin."

"Yuck!" I say.

"But someone else really did torch the place, which could make *me* the prime suspect."

Mira nods. "I'd take that as a warning that it's time to stop being a tease."

"But I can't just turn it off! I swear, I was born a tease…"

Mira closes her eyes again, but only for an instant. When she opens them, she looks at Erik and says, "Keep reminding yourself that the seed is sacred."

That's what Grandfatherly Figure said, didn't he? Or something like that. The seed is sacred. What seed? My children someday? Star children? Feels right. Sounds nice.

"Sacred seed or not, I'm still a freakin' frog. I told Jolie I'd try to change, but—" Erik finishes with his shoulders up in a shrug.

"You're not listening to me," Mira tells him.

"Erik doesn't listen to anyone—" I say, and at the exact same moment a sudden thought makes me interrupt myself. "—but you *can* change, Erik, if you really want to."

"Sorry, but I've got serious doubts and I should know," Erik replies.

Chapter 18 - Last Launch

Last night's dream is coming back full force, no stopping it now.

"You can. I dreamt about you last night, well, not just you, but you were a frog in my dream…"

"Figures," he says.

I smile and start over. "You were a frog in my dream, along with thousands more, maybe even millions, all coming down different paths to the quarry. And it was almost midnight, but still light out, and I saw flames shoot up in every direction around us. I panicked, afraid I couldn't warn everyone in time, but then this peaceful feeling came over me…"

I squeeze my eyes shut, so I can recreate the scene as honestly as possible. "I knew the frogs would be saved as long as they kept moving towards the water. And then they began to jump in, all of them, and their slimy, slippery frog skins dissolved and guess what?"

"They started swimming!" Harry yells out.

"Good guess, but not the right answer," I tell him, my eyes still closed. "What happened is that underneath their slimy skins they were all in white, like brides and grooms."

I open my eyes, almost expecting to see the quarry.

"Soggy ones, I bet," Erik says with a chuckle.

"Like Aunt Tish and Chuck, right, Jojo?" Harry giggles.

Quarry Face

What is it with boys? This is what Aunt Tish would call 'major,' but they're making jokes. I look at Mira and ask, "What do you think it means?"

I don't add my biggest questions of all: How come I'm on the shore watching? Why aren't I in the water with everyone else?

A sudden thud makes me jump. Oh, it's just Marco, thundering down the stairs. I guess Mira won't talk about my dream anymore.

That's okay. From the way this day is going, I figure whatever happens next might be even more interesting than Mira's possible reply.

Chapter 19
A Smudge & A Glimpse

> "Ask the right questions,
> Do not be shy,"
> Whispers the Cosmos;
> "For guides cannot lie."
>   Jolie Rich
>   Carmel, New York

"So was that your sister, Anna, on the phone?" asks Mira.

Marco nods without looking up from loading his slides.

"I'm glad you took lots of pictures of the quarry," Mira says next, instead of asking how his sister is, which is what I'd expect her to say.

Why do I think he's not telling the truth?

"It's what I do. I'm the photographer," Marco replies as he keeps adding slides to his carousel. When he's done, he looks up and says, "I'm hoping you guys can help me decide which slides to put in my book proposal about the quarry. I'm thinking of calling it *Quarry Magic*."

Quarry Face

He's got such a sheepish smile right now. That's terrible of me, not trusting him.

"Is Jojo in them?" Harry asks.

"Of course," Marco says.

"Then call it *Quarry Face*."

We're all laughing while Marco lifts up his projection screen and has Erik pull down the window shades. Then Marco starts leafing through his record albums.

"Can you put on some Dylan?" Mira asks him.

Dylan! I love him, too. Oh, I hope I get a chance to talk to Mira before she leaves. What if I never see her again?

Marco's showing his first slide. It's from the day Erik went to the quarry with us. He looks so cute. Too bad I can't trust him. Now there are a bunch of slides from that same day, one after the other. I blush. "Marco, you took too many shots of me!"

"But your face is perfect for the quarry," Mira says. "You look like a fairytale princess who can turn billions of frogs into princes. I'm serious. You do."

That's silly. Also, I knew it: Marco's slides of the quarry aren't the same as being there.

"I wish I had a time machine and could go back and change everything. Getting kicked out of the quarry is the worst thing that has ever happened to me," I say and can't help but stop to wipe my eyes. "Oh, I'm sorry."

Chapter 19 - A Smudge & A Glimpse

Mira gently squeezes my shoulder. "It'll be all right, Jolie. Really, it will."

"Maybe those guys just pretended to own the place so they could have it to themselves," Erik says. He's standing by the fireplace with his arms crossed.

"Maybe, but I won't take a chance and sneak in again. I told you, they had a *rifle*."

"Women!" Erik says, like being scared is girlish.

He and Marco start laughing. Harry joins in.

"Men!" Mira says to me.

We're all laughing as Marco continues his show. He's got more photos of Erik, me, Harry, and the frogs. He's got some good shots of Mom, too, from the day she came to the quarry. The slides are in random order, so I never know what'll come next.

"Uh oh. Looks like we've reached our last slide," Marco says, right around when I began to fear he'd say that.

"And your long-time curse hurts, but what's worse/Is this pain in here…"

I'm being thrown out of the quarry all over again.

"Not the last slide!" Harry yells and clutches his chest.

I want to always remember Bob Dylan singing and Harry pretending he's been shot and Erik chuckling and Mira sighing, and everything else about this moment, so I can write it down when everyone's gone.

Quarry Face

The screen goes blank. No more bright light. No more whirring fan. Nothing.

"It worked perfectly a second ago," Marco says, flicking on the light switch on the wall.

"But you break just like a little girl."

Marco lowers the music and plugs the projector into a different wall socket. Nothing. He blows on the projector's bulb. Some dust flies, but still nothing. He tries a new bulb. No good.

"Well, at least it waited until the very last slide to conk out," he says.

"Boohoo. I want to see the last slide." Harry rubs his eyes with his fists, pretending to cry.

"Well, I do have a small hand viewer if you don't mind taking turns."

Harry jumps up and claps.

Mira glances from him to me to Erik to her watch.

"I guess I've got time. I'd like to see it, too," she says.

It's happening again, the word 'time' sounding weird, like it belongs to some ancient language.

Marco dashes upstairs and returns with his slide viewer. It's shaped like a small black box, and has a screen on one side with a slot for the slide. He starts wiping it.

"Achoo!" he yells, pretending to sneeze from the dust.

Chapter 19 - A Smudge & A Glimpse

Harry giggles as Marcos slips his last slide into the viewer, turns on its light, and looks at the small screen.

"So far, so good," he says a minute later, while handing the viewer with the slide in it to Mira. "You start. Then pass it on."

I figure Mira will soon look very sad, because the last's the last. Of course, Marco shot some photos today. But I might never want to see those. Too sad.

Mira's staring at the screen. Now she's pulling the viewer closer and staring more. And now she's looking up, grinning.

Grinning?

"You notice anything odd about this slide?" she asks Marco.

"You mean the smudge? The lab screwed up," he replies. "I'll see if they can correct it the next time I'm there."

Still grinning, Mira hands me the viewer.

Harry starts to pout.

"Let your sister see it first," Mira says very gently.

To my surprise Harry doesn't make a fuss.

So it's my turn. I look at the screen like Mira did. Hey, I remember this shot. It's the one Marco took right after he told me and Erik to move closer together on Sunwake. He managed to get the white flower in it, as well as Erik with his arm around me and— I gasp.

Quarry Face

This can't be, can it?

I pull the viewer closer, my arms tingling. I turn to Mira. She's shaking her head very slowly, her expression a lot like Erma's wise-aleck grin that first day we met. A second later I'm grinning, too. Yes, yes, yes.

I nod at Mira and then hand a cookie to Harry and the viewer to Erik.

While Harry munches and Erik focuses, I silently start counting, like I do when I try talking to birds. At 19, Erik looks over to me. He's got the most wonderfully bewildered expression I've ever seen. I put my finger to my lips. He nods.

"Be extra careful with this slide," he tells Harry, while handing him the viewer.

I recognize that face. Harry thinks he's being treated like a kid. I'm guessing he'll be disappointed at first, not seeing any frogs. But he'll be looking for something that's camouflaged, so maybe?

"Huh? What's that? What's there with Jojo and Erik?" he asks.

He made it to 14. Now he's squinting at the screen and shaking the viewer.

"Hey, easy there, mate," says Marco, taking the viewer back from Harry.

He looks into it again.

Chapter 19 - A Smudge & A Glimpse

I glance at Mira. She's watching Marco. She looks like she's praying.

"I've got to tell those guys at the lab to be more careful. Anyway, it's just a smudge," Marco tells us. Then he starts stacking his slides back in their box.

I feel like putting my arm around Mira, she looks so sad. I'm pretty sure I know why. All of us, except for Marco, saw the same thing—a luminous figure between Erik and me. But did they see exactly what I saw? It was no Virgin Mary, that's for sure. It wasn't even human. It was more an energy that can take on any shape it must to convey its message. Without any words being spoken, I can feel *the seed is sacred*. Oh, Erma. I'm going to miss you so! I'd love even just one more glimpse of you, just a glimpse.

Erik's coming over to the couch. He sits down on its arm next to me.

"Mira?" he says.

She turns his way. She still looks sad to me.

"I'm not as dumb as I act," he tells her. "I'll take good care of Princess, here."

"Princess," I softly repeat as Erik touches my shoulder.

I don't get it. How come he's with me now but couldn't be on Sunwake? And what's he mean about taking good care of me? And why couldn't Marco see what the rest of us saw? Maybe letting in some fresh air will clear my mind.

Quarry Face

Marco's collapsing the projection screen as I head for the window.

"*Achoo!*" He sneezes, this time for real. "Oh, excuse me...*aaaaaachooooo!*"

"God bless you," Mira says.

"Yeah, God bless," Erik tells him.

"Gesundheit." Harry and I say in sync, which has us both laughing while I lift up the shade, then the window.

I turn back to the others just as Marco looks like he's about to say, 'Thank you.' But at that exact second, a sudden gust of wind whooshes across my face and tiny bird's feet land on my shoulder still tingling from Erik's touch. Marco's jaw drops. He lifts his camera to his eye.

"Wow," says Harry, jumping up.

From the corner of my eye, I see a brownish bird with a pink crest and red bill inches from my nose.

Am I dreaming?

Not dreaming. Just glimpsing. You get one last glimpse for now.

"It's a female cardinal. The males are much brighter," Marco says, while snapping one photo after another. "This is too good to be true."

Chapter 19 - A Smudge & A Glimpse

"A female cardinal. How absolutely clever," Mira says, her hand on Harry's shoulder. I guess she doesn't want him running over and chasing the bird away.

Hey, I just realized I heard you in my mind, and I'm not in the quarry.

That's right. You did.

I want to ask a zillion questions, but Marco's snapping away, and then he glances at his watch and says, "Mira, you've got to go if you plan to make your flight."

"Maybe I should stay," she replies, staring at me and the cardinal. Then she shakes her head. "No, I can't. But I'm so glad I got to meet all of you as you are right now…"

She gives Harry a hug. He makes a face, like always with strangers, but he's not pulling away. Next, she bends over to hug Erik. He stands up and hugs her back, laughing and looking sweet and shy. Sweet and shy— Erik? Then she walks over to where I'm standing with the bird near the window. She stretches out her hands on either side of us for an imaginary hug.

I'm not going to fall, the bird says.

Mira looks like she didn't hear.

What's that mean?

You'll know when you're ready.

"Marco, can you help me bring down my stuff from upstairs?" Mira asks. Then she heads for the stairs.

Quarry Face

Marco follows, looking over his shoulder until he starts up the staircase.

"Bird still there?" he yells from upstairs.

"Still here," I yell back as Harry inches his way towards me.

Meanwhile, Erik's eyes look as shiny as I hope someone's will someday when I'm older and ready to fall in love and get married. Fall in love? Maybe it should be rise in love. That sounds better. Anyway, I never want to forget Erik's look, or anything about today, especially the cardinal on my shoulder.

Do you have a name? I ask.

Mentor. You can call me Mentor.

I smile. *Mentor? That's a nice name.*

"Mentor," Erik whispers with a smile.

Harry giggles and points to Mentor, "Did your parents name you that?"

They both must have heard the bird! Did they hear me, as well?

Maybe I'll become a vet when I grow up.

That's Harry's thought!

Great idea, I think back.

Chapter 19 - A Smudge & A Glimpse

When I glance to my side, Erik's giving Harry and me a thumbs up, like he heard our thoughts, too.

Just a glimpse, children. Just a glimpse until the stage is set.

I understand, I silently reply (although I doubt I do 100%) and then I'm laughing, we're all laughing, because Harry and Erik thought the exact same thought at the exact same—what for the moment we call—*time.*

Epilogue

After all they'd lived through,
They saw each other anew,
And began to prepare
For guests honored and dear.
   Jolie Adams
   Tucson, Arizona

Sunday, August 21, 2016

Dear Journal,

Today is a very special day, but before I tell you why, let me summarize what led up to it. A lot has happened since that August day in 1985 when Mentor spoke to us, then flew away before Mira and Marco came back downstairs. Marco took Mira's luggage outside, with Erik and Harry following. From Marco's kitchen screen door, Mira and I watched them put her bags into her car. Then Marco checked under its hood and asked Erik to start up the motor. Erik looked like he was having fun.

Mira didn't. Seeing her face, I had to say something.

Epilogue

"I know it's none of my business, but why aren't you and Marco together anymore? I can tell you really like each other."

"We do," Mira said, still staring outside. "I hate leaving him."

"So why are you?"

"I don't have a choice. Maybe you'll understand better when you're older. Maybe I will too," she said, then turned to me with a faint smile. "For now, try to write down what you remember from today, and put it somewhere safe until you get a sign to show it to others."

"I've kept a journal since I was eight."

"I started around that age, too," Mira said.

I love coincidences. But I still had questions. "How will I know a sign's real and not my imagination?"

"If there's one thing I'm sure about, it's that you'll know," Mira said.

She sounded confident.

Marco motioned from outside, and honked the horn.

"It's time to go," Mira said and swung open the screen door.

"Are you sure you can't stay?" I asked, following behind. When she nodded, I asked, "Can I write to you then?"

Mira stopped, turned around, and put her hands on my shoulders.

Quarry Face

"That'll be hard, Jolie. I'll be traveling a lot. Besides, it's best not to communicate about all of this too early. We'll both be safer that way. And when the time comes, I'm sure we'll figure out how to get in touch." She started walking again, then stopped abruptly, and faced me once more. "Just do your best, keep up with your journal, and enjoy your journey."

"My journey? You mean my life?" I asked, as we continued on, this time side by side.

She did.

~

That night, I wrote for hours. I wrote about Erma and Grandfatherly Figure, about Mentor, about getting kicked out of the quarry, and about Marco's last slide. I wrote about my dream with a fire all around while frogs turned into brides and grooms in the water. I made everything into a story, so if anyone found my journal they wouldn't think I'd lost my mind. And when I was all written out, I felt happier than ever. I may have complained before about life being unfair, but that night I felt blessed to have witnessed all that I did. A few days later, when we got back to Brooklyn, I stashed my Carmel journal in the bottom drawer of my bedroom dresser. It stayed there until I was old enough to rent a safe deposit box at a bank.

I didn't get back to Carmel much.

Aunt Tish and Uncle Chuck gave up their cottage in '86, right after their wedding. They live in Vermont now. Their documentary about Medjugorje didn't make much money, although they never regretted making it. They've had more success with other documentaries and with planting hybrids. They have two children, both girls.

Epilogue

A year after my aunt and uncle left Carmel, Erik's family left, too. By then his mom and Big Al were married. Erik gave Big Al his blessings on one condition—that he start baking chocolate chip cookies with walnuts.

They're one of Big Al's biggest sellers on his bakery's website!

My own parents ended their separation before '85 ended. Dad said he'd learned his lesson. Mom said she could see that, and she forgave him. I couldn't. Aunt Tish and Mom kept saying I should "cut him some slack" because he was trying hard not to lose his temper when we disagreed. But I didn't want to risk his words making me doubt myself ever again. I avoided him as much as possible. About seven years after Carmel, he had a sudden heart attack and died. Two years later, Mom met a man who treats her like a queen to this day. Erik's stepdad made all the pastries for their wedding, which got him rave reviews and lots of new customers.

As for Mira, Aunt Tish saw her briefly in Medjugorje. For a few years after that, I heard bits and pieces from my aunt about Mira; how she got married, but not to Marco, and had a daughter, then got divorced. Aunt Tish doesn't know where they live now.

The last time I saw Marco was at his apartment in Greenwich Village, where I took Harry to pick up my free copy of *Quarry Magic* soon after it was published. I was seventeen then. Marco had sold his house in Carmel the winter before. He said he was too busy to make good use of it. He was even too busy to keep his apartment clean! There were cameras, cables, lenses, slides, and lights everywhere. He had to clear a bunch of them off his couch so Harry and I could sit down to skim *Quarry Magic*. Marco's photos were fantastic, but…

Quarry Face

"It's weird to be in so many pictures," I told him.

"You really do have a quarry face!" Harry said.

That got Marco laughing, as he grabbed two photos off a shelf in his living room, and handed them to me.

"These are the prints you wanted," he said.

I'd hoped he'd make them, but he hadn't promised, just said "Uh huh," when I phoned with my request, and not wanting to be a nag, I hadn't bugged him after that.

"Too bad the cardinal couldn't go into *Quarry Magic*, but he wasn't in the quarry, like the rest of the shots," Marco explained, as I looked at the first photo.

I grinned, seeing Mentor on my shoulder. Harry, looking on with me, grinned, too.

Then I looked at the second photo and got the chills. I glanced at Harry. Later he confirmed I'd guessed right; he got goose bumps, too.

"You didn't put this one in the book either," I said, looking up at Marco.

"The lab was never able to get rid of that smudge. But you wanted a print anyway," he said, then added. "I guess you really like that guy."

He meant Erik.

"I guess so," I replied. Maybe I blushed.

Epilogue

After our visit, I framed Mentor's photo. The one of Erik, Erma, and me, I kept with my journal. Over the years, I took it out of my safe deposit box whenever I needed an extra dose of faith. It's lonely carrying around secrets.

I lost track of Marco after our visit. Aunt Tish did, too, until someone she met about a year ago told her to google his website. That's how she found out that he's a celebrity photographer in Los Angeles now, with a wife who's a screenwriter, and three sons. I wonder if he ever thinks about that summer in Carmel.

I know Erik does.

We survived two stupid break-ups before we accepted that we belong together. Once we settled that, if one of us acted like a jerk (Erik far more than me), the other would say, "Remember Carmel." Then we'd be good again. We married soon after I graduated college.

Over the next few years, I tried getting my verses and short stories published, but gave that up after too many rejection slips. I continued working on my writing, though, and I think I've gotten better. Meanwhile, in the 'real world,' I've had a variety of jobs. For a long time I have been the editor for a company that does promotional products, like mugs, t-shirts, stickers, and bookmarks. I'm paid well, the company is ethical, and I figure eventually I'll use the skills I've learned here to promote a new world. I'd have liked to do more conscious preparation for it, but Mentor was very firm in her warning before she flew away. *Don't mess with your mind until the stage is set.*

Two more items and I'll get to why I'm writing so much today.

Quarry Face

First, an update on Medjugorje. For years, I wanted to go there with Erik. Once we had a family, first David, then Eva, I thought we all should go. But first there was the Bosnian War in the area. After that ended, and Medjugorje became part of the Federation of Bosnia and Herzegovina, one thing after another forced us to postpone our trip. Finally, I decided I couldn't force it. When the time to go comes, I'll know it. Meanwhile, the Pope hasn't officially ruled on the visionaries' claims, although it's visited yearly by hundreds of thousands of people, and there are many online reports of miracles, which mean different things to different people, of course.

Secondly, we live in Tucson, Arizona now, because right after Erik got his medical license, he accepted a position at a clinic here. Yes, he's a family doctor! Who'd have guessed! I've seen that with lots of friends; you don't know what people will wind up becoming. Or where they'll live. I never thought I'd like the desert, but it has turned out to be a great place to bring up kids. Not only are the people friendly, and three seasons out of four lovely, but we get to spend many clear nights outside, observing the sky and sharing our thoughts. Up to a point, anyway. I haven't been completely honest with our kids about what happened in Carmel, although they've looked through *Quarry Magic*, and know the place is very special to me.

So, for many years, we were just a typical family here in the sunny Southwest.

That changed forever today.

∼

Feeling a nudge on my arm, I opened my eyes to find Eva staring at my nose cross-eyed, like she's done before to make me laugh. But the clock on my nightstand read 4:34 A.M. I bolted up.

Epilogue

"Don't worry, nothing's wrong," she said, as I turned on my lamp.

"Oh, good," I replied, laughing in relief.

"But I had to come in, Mommy. I had the weirdest dream. I have to tell it to you."

Looking at my fifteen-year-old daughter—exactly fifteen today—I nodded. *Maybe this is it* ran through my mind, and as usual, I shooed that thought away. I'd been disappointed too often in the past.

"So, in my dream I was in a swimming hole," Eva said, "just like that place in *Quarry Magic*, and there was a huge fire in the distance. Really. Flames were all around, but from where I stood, I saw thousands of frogs running down to the water from every direction, and when they reached it—I swear, Mommy, I'm not just making this up—they turned into human beings. Not just human beings, but brides and grooms! Isn't that weird?"

I sensed Erik waking up. I put my hand on his temple. I could feel it pulsating. He knew I'd never told Eva my dream.

"It's not that I was scared," Eva went on, "but it seemed so real, like I was there! I'm sorry, Daddy, I didn't mean to wake you."

"No, that's fine," Erik said, leaning over to turn on his own lamp. Then he lay back down, his hands behind his head, and watched us.

Eva's sparkling eyes reminded me of the sun's rays dancing in the quarry. And my heart suddenly ached for our younger selves—mine, Erik's and Harry's—when we shared a glimpse of things to come.

"I'll be right back. Stay with Daddy for a while," I said, as I slipped out of bed. Trusting that Erik would be great with Eva has always been a joy to me. I've met lots of men who should not be raising kids. Or, at the very least, should take lessons in what being a good father entails.

I quietly closed the sliding glass door behind me. No birds visible in our backyard. Maybe I heard some rustling in the cypress trees, but I couldn't swear to it. That's okay. I wasn't seeking any feathered friends as I looked up, past the treetops, and Earth's almost full moon, to the rest of the universe—more beautiful, mysterious, accessible, and multi-dimensional than humans can yet imagine.

I knew I had to make plans. There was stuff to do for Eva's birthday, of course. But I'd try to phone Harry with my news before he left for his veterinary clinic. And, as soon as possible, I'd retrieve my journal and photo from my safe deposit box. Even sooner, I'd start searching for Mira. If it's been a long journey for me, it's been even longer for her. But then, I suppose it's all a drop in the cosmic bucket, isn't it?

Most importantly, I'd figure out what to tell Eva and when. I don't want to scare her, but we've got to talk. Ever since she was a toddler, I've felt she'd be the first to share my secret, but I wasn't sure when until now. Eva's dream was my sign. How perfect that it came on her fifteenth birthday. I was fifteen when I felt contacted in Carmel. Mira was fifteen, too.

Eva's got a lot ahead of her; learning how to develop her gifts, recognize fellow travelers, and protect herself and her kind. Whether from fear or ignorance, or because it's the natural way evolution works, she'll face dangers that must be

Epilogue

overcome, so that her seed can flourish, and take advantage of the energy being made available. Earth's future depends on it.

And no doubt, like all Earthlings, Eva will need a guide. That part should be easy.

I meditated on that last dream I had in Carmel for years before I accepted the truth. I'm a guide. That's why I stood on the shore while all the frogs splashed into the water. I don't know how many other guides Earth has, maybe millions, maybe just a few, but once they start waking up, we should be able to connect. You can't fake receiving. And I'm sure Eva will be a guide, too. I'm less sure what role our son, David plays, but Eva's dream confirms what I suspected from way back when she was a toddler; sharper, more inquisitive, and caring than others her age. Perhaps it won't take her as much time as it took me to accept her role. Time. That pesky word still double dares me to define it.

Enough for now! From the reddening sky, I guess it's an hour till sunrise. Of course, I feel like running off and writing poetry, but I know I have lots to do first. A smile crosses my face as I continue gazing at the sky, and though I have no scientific proof yet where my gratitude goes, I silently say, *Thank you for sending a new story to Earth.*

With that, I send up an air kiss to the heavens. Then I head back inside for the first day of The Cosmic Age.

About the Author

Karen Mitnick Liptak is a native New Yorker, Brooklyn College graduate, and the author of many nonfiction books, primarily for children and young adults. These include *Out In The Night, Dating Dinosaurs And Other Old Things, Native American Sign Language,* and *Endangered Peoples.* A former documentary filmmaker with Newsreel and PBS in New York, and an Editorial Director for Positive Promotions, she's currently a tour guide at Kitt Peak National Observatory, near Tucson, Arizona, where she offers visitors scientific facts and a cosmic perspective.

www.ingramcontent.com/pod-product-compliance
Lightning Source LLC
LaVergne TN
LVHW021713060526
838200LV00050B/2646